Feline Folk Tales

Feline Folk Tales

ANNA MARIA VILHELMINA
HELLBERG MOBERG

The History Press

First published 2026

The History Press
97 St George's Place, Cheltenham,
Gloucestershire, GL50 3QB
www.thehistorypress.co.uk

British Library Cataloguing in Publication Data.
A catalogue record for this book is available from the British Library.

ISBN 978 1 80399 972 2

Typesetting and origination by The History Press
Printed and bound in Great Britain by TJ Books, Padstow, Cornwall.

MIX
Paper | Supporting responsible forestry
FSC® C013056
www.fsc.org

The History Press proudly supports
Trees for Life
www.treesforlife.org.uk

EU Authorised Representative: Easy Access System Europe
Mustamäe tee 50, 10621 Tallinn, Estonia
gpst.request@easproject.com

Dedicated to cat lovers everywhere and, of course, to some of my favourite feline companions:

Randi – my very first cat companion until I developed cat allergies aged seven.

Bessie – who moved in and miraculously cured those allergies nearly thirty years later.

Bowie – my current 'cat share' (with my neighbour).

And to all the fabulous felines I've been looking after these last fifteen years, including Oluf in Denmark, Mum in Spain, Bouda, aka Boudicca, and Jumbie, and the Magnificent 7 (especially Jumeirah, Tinkerbell, Nelson and Habibi) in the United Kingdom, and the London kitties: Jeffrey, Mowgli and Aurora, Pepe, Mochi, Solo, Bella, Shadow, Maggie, Póg, Fluffy Marie, Smithy, Steed and Mrs Peel, Atticus and Booma, Hamish, Lucky and Eddie, and many, many other gorgeous kittycats.

CONTENTS

INTRODUCTION

I've been a firm ailurophile all my life, but it's only in the last two decades I've been able to give my love of cats free rein. At the age of seven, my parents finally gave in to my pleas and agreed we could get a cat. We had just moved from a smalltown flat to a countryside home in a tiny community in western Sweden and that summer, Randi moved in with us. I loved her! Or him, as it turned out upon closer inspection and he had to be spayed. We were bonding beautifully, but then – shock, horror – a few months down the line I started developing quite severe cat allergies and thus had to part with Randi forever. My parents told me he had 'moved to Lapland', hundreds of miles from where we lived, and even as an adult, I confess I never dared to approach the subject and learn the truth about his fate.

My cat allergies remained severe throughout my childhood, teenage years and into adulthood. Much as I loved cats, I came to the sad conclusion that I would never be able to get close to them and enjoy their company. Then, in my mid-30s, something extraordinary happened. An acquaintance was moving abroad and couldn't find anyone who would adopt his cat, Bessie, so he asked my flatmate and me to help. Would Bessie be able to move in with us?

I was *very* hesitant, but in the end agreed to let her move in. The first few weeks involved plenty of antihistamine and tissues, the odd use of my inhaler, but guess what? As I got used to Bessie, my allergies started to settle down and, slowly but surely, to disappear. For the first time in nearly thirty years, I was able to enjoy feline company and plenty of cuddles without streaming nose and eyes and constant wheezing. I was cured!

I had always been something of a 'closet mad cat lady', and allergies gone, let's just say I have now firmly entered what I hope will be a lifelong 'cat phase', both as a person and a writer. The last fifteen years or so, cat-sitting jobs have taken me to many different parts of the United Kingdom and Europe, while at home in London, I work for the agency Love Cats (love-cats.uk) on a regular basis.

Cats have also been sauntering, leaping and pouncing their way into my writing for over a decade. In 2015 I penned *Cats, A Miscellany* for Summersdale (writing as Anna Maria Espsäter) and several of my works of fiction, such as *How Pat Got Her Five Cats*, *How Pat Met the Curry-Cat* and *Hug-Snow Days*, feature plenty of felines. *Feline Folk Tales* feels like a natural progression both from a professional and personal point of view and I was delighted that The History Press liked my book idea. Initially I thought of *Supremely Cute Killers* as a good title, but as this book covers cats big as well as small, wild as well as tame, I decided they might not all be deemed cute.

Cats inspire love and affection, awe and admiration, curiosity and fascination – not to mention fear, suspicion, even hatred – but they rarely leave us unmoved. From the fearsome roar of a lion to a plaintive meow, ferocious hiss or thunderous purr, our feline friends have a tremendous repertoire of evocative sounds. They can be loyal or fickle, friendly, greedy, lazy, protective and destructive in equal measure, but ultimately, at least for this author, their endearing qualities always outweigh their sometimes less than 'sweetness-and-light' behaviour. Supremely cute they may be, but with remnants of a truly wild streak lurking underneath the surface.

This book brings together over fifty feline folk tales from all over the world, some in print for the first time, some translated from Swedish and Spanish. In many of the stories, cats – big and small, wild and domesticated – take centre stage, but even in the tales where they share the stage with others, their presence is always felt. As cat owners well know, cats rule the world – and the home (and the internet – hilarious kitten videos, need I say more?). While dogs follow, cats lead.

On these pages, you'll meet the cat both as hero/heroine and villain. Stories of classy cats, curious cats, cunning cats, clever cats, shapeshifters and demons, greedy gluttons and bold *bon vivants*, prowl the book from cover to cover. Selfish, self-serving, untrustworthy and downright vicious cats are contrasted with sweet, caring, funny and loving moggies. In my research I've come across almost as many cute tales as cruel ones and this duality holds true globally. The theory that cats became domesticated while in search of an easy meal is one that, to be honest, I can well believe. Cats, on the whole, however independent they may seem, are often on the lookout for not just an easy meal, but an easy life, and if purring and being sweet to humans get them what they want ... well, it's a sacrifice they're willing to make. On their own terms.

The book is divided geographically into Africa, the Americas, Australasia and Europe, and each geographical section has its own short introduction. As this book's focus is the domestic cat and many African folk tales are focused on their wilder relations, the Africa section is a little shorter than the others. Australia, New Zealand and the Pacific Islands have been combined with Asia, as again, I've not come across enough domestic cat tales from this region for obvious reasons; cats only appeared on many of these shores with the arrival of Europeans in the eighteenth century (see the 'Superstitions, Sayings and Ships' Cats' chapter, page 165). Some countries or regions stand out – with places jampacked with ailurophiles, such as Japan – while in other places, cat tales are fewer and further between. Europe is the section with the most folk tales focused on the domestic cat, and in consequence, it is the longest chapter. It's also the only one where there are no big cats, unless you count the bear in the Norwegian tale (see 'The Kitty of Dovrefjell Mountain', page 126).

Cats, big and small, crop up in myths and legends from all over the world as well, which is why I felt they merited their very own chapter (see 'Cats in Myths and Legends', page 159); Celtic and Norse, Greek and Roman, Native American and First Nation, Egyptian and Hebrew, Persian, Thai, Chinese and Japanese mythology all have a sprinkling of fine felines. There is a fine line between a myth and a folk tale, so I have included some full-length tales that are arguably myths, while others simply get a mention in the chapter specifically dedicated to myths and legends. As there are many superstitions and sayings associated with cats, these too get their own chapter, combined with a swift glance at the importance of ships' cats (see pages 165–173).

Throughout this last year of cat research I have been pleasantly surprised by the many wondrous and wonderful cat tales I have come across, from such different corners of the world as Brazil and Taiwan. I hope the reader enjoys delving, or alternatively dipping, into this collection of feline folk tales as much as I have enjoyed compiling it.

Anna Maria Vilhelmina Hellberg Moberg
London, 25 August 2025

A FURTHER NOTE ON THE CONTENT OF THIS BOOK

Some people today equate folk tales with fairy tales and assume they are all meant for children, but this could hardly be further from the truth. Throughout history, people have invented, created and recounted tales for all occasions, for adults as well as children. Folk tales are no exception and, while some are funny and fantastical, others contain elements that are dark, gory and downright brutal. As a result, this collection contains material and language that might not be suitable for young readers.

FELINE FOLK TALES OF AFRICA

African feline folk tales, as you'll discover, have a tendency to feature big cats rather than small, despite ample evidence of the importance of cats on African soil, especially in Egypt (theories about the time and place of the domestication of cats vary – see also 'Cats in Myths and Legends', page 159). That said, folk tales from across the continent feature cats of both sizes, sometimes even in the same story. In many of the African tales, cats, whether big or small, domesticated or wild, appear in combination with other animals – for example, monkey, gazelle or tortoise. Although often portrayed as cunning and self-serving, cats don't always get their own way in these tales and are sometimes outsmarted by other animals – or by humans.

This chapter features a selection of different folk tales – humorous tales, horror stories, cautionary tales, explanatory tales – where cats are key players, from places as far apart as Zambia, Morocco and Nigeria. Some are mere snippets – short and sweet, or not so sweet, as it happens – some longer. As the focus of the book is on the humble (or arguably regal) domestic cat, rather than big cats, this section is a little shorter than the other geographical divisions.

THE OBSTINATE CHILD

Berber Folk Tale, Maghreb Region, Northern Africa

There are many stories of wilful or stubborn children in folk and fairy tales. One such example is the story of the wilful child collected by the Brothers Grimm (Tale No. 117 – 'The Wilful Child'). In this tale of Berber origin, it is ultimately the cat that holds the key to the story by, unusually, obeying an order, rather than refusing to comply (the latter could arguably be deemed more 'catlike' behaviour).

'Child, eat your dinner,' Child was told, but Child refused.
'Stick, beat child,' Stick was told, but Stick refused.
'Fire, burn stick,' Fire was told, but Fire refused.
'Water, quench fire,' Water was told, but Water refused.
'Ox, drink water,' Ox was told, but Ox refused.
'Knife, kill ox,' Knife was told, but Knife refused.
'Blacksmith, break Knife,' Blacksmith was told, but Blacksmith refused.
'Rope, hang Blacksmith,' Rope was told, but Rope refused.
'Rat, gnaw Rope,' Rat was told, but Rat refused.
'Cat, eat Rat,' Cat was told and …
'Gladly!' said Cat.
Cat scared Rat, who scared the Rope, which scared the Blacksmith, who scared the Knife, which scared the Ox, who scared the Water, which scared the Fire, which scared the Stick, which scared the Child. And the Child ate her dinner.

THE CAT WHO CAME INDOORS

Tanzania, Southern Africa, Brazil

There are many different versions of the story of how cats became domesticated – some from eastern Africa (such as this one), some from southern Africa, and there's even one from Brazil (see The Americas section, pages 31–54). Arguably, the tale shows the cat to be a cunning, fickle, calculating and self-serving sort of creature, but also admirably adaptable, becoming domesticated by choice, while retaining a wild streak. This is one of a few tales I've come across to include all sorts of different animals, and the odd human or two.

Once upon a time, there was a wildcat, living all by herself in the bush. As time went on, this cat got rather tired of living alone and so she took herself a husband. This husband was a wildcat also and she thought he was the finest creature in all the land.

One day, as they were walking together along the path through the tall, rich grass, Leopard suddenly leapt out at them from the high, swaying greenery and Wildcat's husband was knocked over and tumbled down into the dust.

'Oooooh!' said Wildcat. 'My husband is all covered in dust and certainly isn't the very finest creature in all the land as I thought. No, it is Leopard.'

And so Wildcat went to live with Leopard.

The pair of them lived together very happily until they were out hunting in the bush one day, when suddenly, out of the shadows there came a great roar and out leapt Lion. Lion landed firmly and ferociously on Leopard's back, and roared, tore and ripped him to shreds, before eating him up.

'Oooooh!' said Wildcat. 'Leopard certainly isn't the very finest creature in all the land as I thought. No, it is Lion.'

And so Wildcat went to live with Lion.

Wildcat and Lion lived together very happily until they were out stalking in the forest one day, when a formidable shape came looming up ahead. With one swift movement, Elephant placed one foot on top of Lion and completely flattened him.

'Oooooh!' said Wildcat. 'Lion certainly isn't the very finest creature in all the land as I thought. No, it is Elephant.'

And so Wildcat went to live with Elephant, climbing up onto his back and sitting there purring on his neck, right between his large, flapping ears.

Wildcat and Elephant lived together very happily until they were moving through the tall reeds down by the river one day when there was a loud bang and Elephant toppled over and sank to the ground. Wildcat looked around, but all she could see was a small man holding a shiny gun.

'Oooooh!' said Wildcat. 'Elephant certainly isn't the very finest creature in all the land as I thought. No, it is Man.'

And so Wildcat followed Man all the way to his home, where she jumped up onto the thatch of his hut.

'At last,' Wildcat said to herself, 'I have found the finest creature in all the land.'

Wildcat made her home very happily up in the thatch of the hut, catching mice and rats that lived in the village. One day, as she was sitting on the roof warming herself in the sun, there was a sudden noise from inside the hut. It was the voices of Man and his wife and the voices were growing louder and louder until finally Man came tumbling head over heels into the dust. He had been kicked out.

'A-ha!' said Wildcat to herself. 'Now I know for sure who is truly the finest creature in all the land. It is Woman.'

Wildcat left 'wild' behind up on the thatched roof, went inside the hut and sat herself down by the fire, purring. That has been her home ever since.

THE CATS AND THE MICE

Ethiopia

Cats as cunning and untrustworthy creatures is a theme in many, many folk tales from all different parts of the world. Here's one from Ethiopia that tells the tale of how cats and mice, who were once good friends, rather fell out when one started eating the other (and it's not hard to work out who ate who).

This might come as a surprise to you, but many, many moons ago, cats and mice used to live together in perfect harmony. It's true, they were good friends. Until the mice began to realise that something mysterious was happening, that is. You see, lots of mice had started to disappear, one by one …

There was nothing for it, the mice had to start investigating what was going on. That's when they realised that it was their 'good friends' the cats who were eating the mice. And so, they came to the sad conclusion that they would have to go into hiding. The mice began digging deep holes that they could stay inside, and mothers always warned their young children not to go anywhere near their former friends, the cats. All the mice hid so well in their holes that as time passed, there were no more mice left for the cats to eat.

This did not please the cats at all, so they got together and began to scheme.

'Listen,' said one of them, 'there are no mice to eat anymore. What can we do about it? How do we lure them out of their hiding places so that we can catch them and eat them?'

They talked and debated for quite some time and then they came up with a cunning plan – a great wedding plan, whereby a son of the cats would marry a daughter of the mice. They'd throw a big wedding party and eat all the mice that would be invited as guests.

The cats sent their elders to the elders of the mice, explaining that they wanted one of their own sons to marry one of the daughters of the mice. Needless to say, the mice were mightily suspicious of this plan.

'No, no, no,' they said, 'we're not interested in this marriage idea of yours. You're not serious, you'll soon eat us all up.'

'No, no, please, forgive us for our past actions and please believe us, we are indeed in earnest and very serious now,' the cats entreated. 'We honestly want this wonderful marriage between our cat son and your mouse daughter.'

They pleaded and cajoled and used their very best persuasion tactics and at long last, the mice relented, and the wedding day was agreed upon.

On the very day of the wedding, the mice were still feeling cautious and apprehensive, so they warned all their children to be careful when the cats arrived and to be on their guard in case there were any problems. The cats were coming, and you could hear them from afar meowing a wedding song. They had changed the words to 'Surround them and swallow them whole, surround them and swallow them whole'.

The mice, in turn, were singing, 'Sing, but keep an eye on the cats, sing, but keep an eye on the cats.'

Then when the mice heard that the cats were singing, 'Swallow them whole', they all jumped back into their holes, all the while singing, 'Keep an eye on the cats, keep an eye on the cats', and so the mice escaped unscathed.

A few days later the elders of the cats returned to speak to the elders of the mice.

'Look, we came to the wedding, but no one showed up,' said the cat elders, all in a huff.

But the mice were unmoved. 'We have grown wise to your tricks,' said they, 'and we will always keep our means of escape.'

The moral of the story is, always keep an emergency exit handy in times of trouble.

THE TORTOISE AND HIS DEBTS

Southern Nigeria

In this rather gruesome Calabar story from southern Nigeria, it's the tortoise who takes centre stage and has the last laugh of all in a moment of pure schadenfreude. As you will see, neither big cat nor wildcat fare too well.

There was once a Tortoise who owed all his friends money and, of course, they were all soon clamouring to get their money back.

'Pay me!' said Worm.

'Just wait here and you will get paid,' Tortoise replied, and then went along to see Rooster.

'Pay me!' said Rooster.

'Just come with me and you will get paid,' Tortoise replied.

So Rooster followed Tortoise, ate Worm, and patiently waited for his money.

But Tortoise was cunning and sneaked off to Wildcat.

'Pay me!' said Wildcat.

'Just come with me and you will get paid,' Tortoise replied.

Wildcat followed Tortoise, ate Rooster, and patiently waited for his money.

Still as cunning as ever, Tortoise then went right along to see Leopard.

'Pay me!' said Leopard.

'Just come with me and you will get paid,' Tortoise replied.

Leopard followed Tortoise and attacked Wildcat. The pair of them fought so fiercely, madly and ferociously that they killed each other in the struggle that ensued.

Tortoise just laughed and then ate them both.

Needless to say, he didn't pay anybody.

THE WILDCAT AND THE GAZELLE

The Democratic Republic of Congo

There's no shortage of brutal and gruesome folk tales involving deception, trickery and cunning. In many, different species start off as good friends, but then something goes wrong … More often than not, it's due to the cat's deceitful behaviour, but every once in a while, a tale appears where it's another animal that can't be trusted. Arguably, in this tale from the Democratic Republic of Congo, explaining why the wildcat and the gazelle are sworn enemies, the two protagonists are as bad as each other.

Wildcat and Gazelle were the best of friends. In fact, they were so close and such good pals that they vowed to each other that if famine ever came, they would eat each other's mothers.

As fate would have it, famine did come to their area and it was time to keep their vow to each other. First the two friends killed and ate Wildcat's mother, but Gazelle was sneaky and he hid his own mother in a nearby cave.

'Now mother,' he said to her, 'please stay here and hide until I call you. Whatever you do, do not come out before I tell you that it is safe.'

But Wildcat was sneaky too, and he soon discovered Gazelle's secret. As soon as Gazelle was gone, Wildcat went to the cave and, imitating Gazelle's voice, cried out, 'You can come on out now, Mother, all is safe!'

As soon as Gazelle's mother stepped out of the cave, Wildcat dealt her a fierce blow that killed her instantly and then he prepared a great feast, inviting Gazelle as the guest of honour. They had a wonderful meal – Gazelle had rarely tasted anything so delicious – and it wasn't until much later that he discovered his mother was missing. Now he understood where the succulent meat from the feast came from. It is rumoured that from that day onwards, Wildcat and Gazelle have been sworn enemies.

THE WILDCAT AND THE NIGHTJAR

Zambia

Another tale focusing on friendship between two species – a cat and a bird, in this case – breaking down due to the cat's devious behaviour. Cats being depicted as cunning and ruthless creatures, not to be trusted, is a theme that's prevalent in many folk tales from around the world, such as in this Kaonde story from Zambia. In some tales kitty gets away with murder and in some kitty gets his/her comeuppance.

Although you might find this hard to believe, as it happened, Wildcat and Nightjar were the very best of friends. Then one day, when Nightjar least expected it, Wildcat began to change her demeanour and started growling at her in a most fearsome manner.

'I'm going to eat you, I'm going to eat you,' she growled, over and over again, hissing and giving Nightjar a tremendous scare.

Nightjar was terrified and, desperately flapping her wings, she fluttered away in fear.

Then Wildcat let out a wild, wicked laugh. 'I was only joking, my dear friend,' she said. 'I didn't mean to scare you. But now let me be serious for a moment. You see, the truth is I'm not quite myself and I'm terribly worried. One of my kittens is gravely ill. If I could have two or three of your feathers to try and make some medicine to cure her, I'd be ever so grateful. I could really use your help.'

Nightjar felt much reassured and gladly gave up some of her feathers to Wildcat. 'Of course, I understand and I'm very happy to help you, my friend,' she said and then they parted ways in friendship just as before.

The very next day, Wildcat made the same request. Her poor little kitten was still sick, she said and she really, really needed another couple of feathers, if Nightjar would be so kind. Then the next day again, the same thing happened, and the next, and the next, and the next. Many days went by and finally, poor Nightjar had given up so many of her feathers that sadly, she had none left and so she was unable to fly away.

That's when her good friend Wildcat, who had cunningly bided her time, grabbed Nightjar and ate her up.

THE WILDCAT AND THE MONKEY

Ghana

A short tale from Ghana explaining how monkeys came to live in trees, all thanks to Wildcat. In a role reversal, the cat in this tale falls victim to the cunning of the monkey, while the monkey escapes the cunning of the cat.

It had been a long night of hunting and Wildcat was exhausted after all her exertions, so she lay down to rest, but she could find no sleep as fleas kept pestering her and biting her all over her body.

That's when she spotted Monkey and asked for his help to get rid of the pesky critters. 'Help me, Monkey, please help me,' she groaned in distress. 'Come and pluck these vicious fleas off me.'

'I will help you gladly,' Monkey replied, and he started plucking as quickly as he could.

As Monkey plucked the fleas, at last Wildcat could get some sleep. But Monkey was not to be trusted.

Almost as soon as Wildcat fell asleep, he stopped plucking. While Wildcat snoozed soundly, Monkey took her tail and tied it to a tree. Then, to wake her up, he whacked her on the head and skipped away, laughing. Wildcat tried to chase after Monkey, but then realised that she was stuck, her tail tied to the tree, and she had no choice but to stay put.

'Just you wait and see, Monkey,' she shouted after him. 'I will get you for this, mark my words.'

Wildcat was mightily angry and really wanted revenge, so she summoned all the animals in the kingdom. There was no shortage of those who had an axe to grind and hated Monkey for all the tricks he always played on friends and foes alike.

'This is what you must do, my friends,' Wildcat told all the animals. 'Announce that I have died and let Monkey know that you will be arranging my funeral, then invite him to the funeral feast.'

Before the funeral guests made their appearance, Wildcat took up her position, lying down and pretending to be dead. All the animals, including Monkey, danced the funeral dance around her body, chanting as they danced.

'*Wildcat is dead, dead, dead …*' they sang.

Then, quick as a flash, Wildcat leapt up, making a grab for Monkey, but Monkey proved to be quicker still and had already escaped to the nearest tree, where he climbed higher and higher, so Wildcat could not reach him.

Ever since that day, Monkeys have always lived in trees.

THE CAT AND THE LEOPARD (Or Why the Leopard Can Only Catch Prey on Its Left Side)

Ghana

There are different versions of this type of story from many parts of the world (for example, the Brazilian tale, 'The Cat's Leap', in The Americas section, page 50). In domestic versus big cat tales, the common moggie is very often more cunning than their wilder cousins, never quite teaching them all their tricks and always keeping something up their sleeve.

Going way back in time, Leopard didn't know how to hunt and catch prey. Cat, on the other hand, was very skilful. Leopard, wanting to learn from the great hunter Cat, went to see him and very politely asked whether Cat would be willing to teach him all his tricks. And so it was that Cat came to teach the art of hunting to Leopard.

Having made an agreement, the very next day, they had their first lesson. Cat taught Leopard the first key trick – how to hide in the bushes – and then the second most important trick – how to move about quite noiselessly. This way, Leopard would be able to stalk his prey without the prey ever knowing it was being followed.

'Look,' said Cat, 'you stalk like this.' Then Cat showed Leopard how best to stalk his prey by stalking a mouse.

'The third trick I'm going to teach you,' said Cat, 'is just as important. You use your left paw and left side like this, to spring upon your prey that's passing you on your left.' Cat demonstrated by killing the mouse.

Leopard, being a fast learner, soon caught his first prey.

'Very good,' said Cat. 'You have mastered the first three tricks in this lesson. Now go off and practise and then come back to me. Next, I'll teach you how to use your right paw and right side to catch prey that's passing you on your right.'

Leopard practised and did well, but soon afterwards he became impatient for his next important lesson. So eager did he become that he went off to Cat's house, hoping his next lesson might start there and then. Sadly, Cat wasn't home, but as it happened, all her little kittens were there, waiting for her. Leopard, feeling quite proficient after his first lesson, practised his skills on the kittens and swiftly ate them all up.

When Cat found out what had happened, she became furious and point-blank refused to give Leopard any more lessons. This is why Leopard is only able to catch prey from the left, not from the right.

NUNDA, THE EATER OF PEOPLE

Swahili Tale, Zanzibar and Coastal Areas of Tanzania

Cats in folk tales, it has to be said, aren't always cuddly, but few are as fierce and ferocious as the cat in this tale. The Nunda, *sometimes known as* Mngwa, *is known for eating people and there are various shorter and longer versions of this story. The best known was collected by Edward Steere in the 1800s and published as* Swahili Tales *in 1870.*

The cat of Sultan Majnún was unusually fierce. One day it killed a calf, but the Sultan dismissed the event, simply stating, 'The cat is mine, and so is the calf'. He could see no problem at all.

The cat then proceeded to kill and eat a goat, followed by a cow, a donkey, a horse and even a camel, with the good Sultan shrugging it off each time. 'I will not kill it, even if it were to eat a man,' the Sultan proclaimed.

And sure enough, the cat killed a human child next and followed this with a fully grown man. By this time, the creature had grown large and monstrous on its diet of human flesh.

Much to everyone's relief, it then left town, but no sooner had the townspeople breathed a sigh of relief than the troubles with the people-eating creature started up again. You see, the Sultan's cat had taken to hiding in the undergrowth, just outside the city limits, and there it feasted on anyone who passed by, whether human or animal. After sunset, it would sneak along the dark roads and abduct hapless wanderers.

Sultan Majnún, however, was still refusing to see the danger. 'You all want me to kill this cat. But I say to you that this is my cat and everything it eats is mine also.' He refused to address the complaints from his citizens and slowly but surely the population of the town continued to dwindle. Anyone and anything not locked up indoors was at risk.

Time went by until one day Sultan Majnún went out to admire the countryside with six of his sons, where the cat lay in wait. As soon as they were passing, the cat attacked them and killed three of the Sultan's sons.

At long, long last, Sultan Majnún came to his senses. 'That is no longer my cat,' he said firmly. 'That is a *Nunda*, and it will eat even me if I give it a chance.'

He sent his soldiers to kill the *Nunda*, but catching and killing a *Nunda* is no easy task. Instead, it killed some of the soldiers, while all the ones remaining fled in fear, escaping the *Nunda*.

Sultan Majnún's seventh son, who'd heard of the terrible havoc and carnage wreaked by the creature, swore a solemn oath that he would slay it. 'I shall find the *Nunda* who killed my brothers,' he told his mother, setting out all alone, with his spear and his knife.

The young prince was nothing if not zealous. The first vaguely intimidating creature he ran into was a large dog, which he promptly killed and dragged home.

'*Mamá, wee, niulága nundá mla wátu!*' he sang triumphantly. ('O mother, I have killed the *Nunda*, eater of people!')

But his mother shook her head sadly and said, 'My son, this is not he, the *Nunda*, eater of people. The *Nunda* is much, much larger than this.'

The seventh son set out again and in turn he managed to first kill a civet, then a larger civet, a zebra, a giraffe, a rhinoceros and finally an elephant, bringing each one back home with him, only to have his mother tell him that these were not the *Nunda*.

In time, he gathered a small group of followers, and with their help, managed to piece together a better description of the *Nunda*: elephant-sized or larger with small ears, broad, but not long, with two blotches like a civet, and a very thick tail.

At long last, the youth's efforts paid off. The *Nunda* was found asleep in the shade of a grove of trees. This undoubtedly was the *Nunda*; it fitted his mother's description of it perfectly and did not resemble anything else he had killed so far.

He and his companions fired their guns into the *Nunda* at close range, but did not hang around for fear that it was still alive. Instead, they slept through the night and returned in the morning when it was determined that the huge cat was undeniably dead.

They dragged the beast back to the town in triumph with the prince singing of his victory, and this time his mother chanted back, '*Mwanangu, ndiyeye nundá mla watu!*' ('My son, this is he, the *Nunda*, eater of people!')

The *Nunda*'s carcass was buried, a house was built on top of it, and a guard was placed at the house.

This is but one tale of the insatiable *Nunda*, a 'swallowing monster'. Sometimes, it swallows the entire populace of a place, with the exception of one lone hero. This hero kills the *Nunda* and cuts it open, releasing all its victims unharmed.

FELINE FOLK TALES OF THE AMERICAS

Once upon a time, there were sabretooth tigers roaming the American continent, and these were followed by the cougar (also known as mountain lion, puma or panther). Domestic cats are a relatively recent addition to the Americas, and are thought to have first arrived onboard the ships of European colonisers. The American continent thus provides a perfect mix of big and small felines appearing in a wide variety of folk tales.

Many tales from across the United States feature domestic kittycats but also wildcats and even occasionally lions; the lynx appears in First Nation tales from Canada (and Native American tales across the border); Native American tales often include wildcats, bobcats and cougars. Werecats crop up in different parts of the region, such as in the story of *El Hombre Gato* from Argentina or the Wampus Cat in the United States. In Mexico and southwestern United States you might meet the Cactus Cat, who loves to get tipsy on fermented cactus juice, aka *mezcal*, and further south, in Brazil, the tales feature the mighty jaguar. In a tale from Haiti, in the Caribbean, a cat is even responsible for striking a deal with God, while another tale crosses continents with a Brazilian version of a well-known African tale, explaining how cats became domesticated in the first place.

Cats of different kinds appear as tricksters, guardians and protectors, shapeshifters or even divine beings across the continent.

WILDCAT GETS A NEW FACE

Ute, Native American, United States

A Native American wildcat versus coyote tale from the Ute people of Colorado, New Mexico and Utah (the name of the latter is derived from the Ute people). Historically, their territory also included parts of Wyoming, Nevada and Arizona.

Long, long ago, Wildcat had a long nose and tail.

One day, he was sleeping on a rock when Coyote came along. He pushed Wildcat's nose and tail in, then he returned home. At noon, Wildcat woke up and noticed his short nose and tail.

'What's the matter with me?' he asked himself, but then he understood. 'Oh, I see. Coyote did this to me!' he said and then he began to hunt for Coyote.

Now it was Coyote's turn to feel sleepy and he lay down to rest. Wildcat sneaked up and came to sit beside him. He pulled out Coyote's nose and tail and made them long. They were short before. And then Wildcat ran off.

After a while, Coyote woke up and saw his long nose and tail. And so it was that Wildcat and Coyote both got new faces.

THE DANCE OF THE *TANGARÁS*

The Pantanal, Brazil

This is a jaguar tale from the tropical wetlands and grasslands of the Pantanal region in Brazil, close to the Paraguayan and Bolivian borders. The tangará *is a colourful bird, native to several South American countries, including Brazil, and is well known for the intricate choreography of its mating dance which, in this tale, is used to outwit the big cat.*

Once upon a time, there was a cunning, young jaguar who was always trying to catch birds, but the birds were quicker and so always managed to fly away, eluding the jaguar's valiant attempts to catch them. One day, however, luck was with him, and he was able to catch a tiny bird. So small was the bird that the jaguar swallowed him whole, beautiful plumage and all. This was a stroke of luck for the bird, who remained alive and well, fluttering about deep inside the jaguar's stomach.

Meanwhile, all the other birds were extremely worried about the fate of their poor friend who had been caught by the jaguar. They had seen him pounce and swallow the bird whole, so they suspected the tiny bird might still be alive in the jaguar's belly, but what could they do? The jaguar was so very big and so very powerful, while they were so very small and so very insignificant.

Feeling deeply saddened and ever so powerless, the birds near enough gave up there and then, without a fight – but suddenly, as one, they rallied. Something had to be done, but they were out of their depth, and they needed some advice.

The flock of birds went to see the owl, the cleverest of all the bewinged creatures, and she had an idea. She told them to call the *tangará* birds and ask them if they could perform their fabulous mating dance in front of the jaguar, who was perched contentedly high up a tree. The birds were delighted with this suggestion so, said and done, they flew off to consult the *tangarás*, who were more than happy to help with the bird-rescuing mission.

Before long, all the *tangarás* were gathered for their ritual dance and, taking to the branches of the very tree where the jaguar was sitting – but not too close, mind you – they began their display. In an instant, the air was abuzz with sound and movement, electrified by the dazzling performance of the *tangarás*.

The jaguar watched this whirlwind of stunning colours, reluctantly at first, then increasingly mesmerised. Unable to stop himself, he opened his mouth wide to express his admiration in a long, drawn-out 'Wooooooooooooooooooow!' and the tiny bird flew out and escaped back to freedom.

LION BROOKS NO RIVAL

African-American, United States

An African-American version of 'The Lion and the Hare' story (see Australasia section, page 58). There are many similar stories, where the big cat doesn't fare so well, particularly from across Asia.

Lion was supposed to be the head of all the beasts in that place. He got so lazy that he had an animal come in ev'ry day so he could eat it. Ev'ryday an animal went in to the lion.

Finally it was the rabbit's turn to go in. He was one of the wisest animals of that time. He was supposed to be there at twelve o'clock.

He came hoppin' along the road, stoppin' everywhere, lookin' at everything, until it threw him off time. Now, what could he do to keep the lion from gettin' so angry with him?

The rabbit finally came across a well. The thought came to him as he looked into the well and saw his own shader, that now he had a scheme to fool the lion. He had been told by the other animals that any way he could get rid of the lion, they would pay him and give him praise of being the wisest animal of the forest.

He entered the lion's den pretendin' he had been runnin', doin' all he could to get there on time. The lion asked him why he was so late. The rabbit began to tell him the story of why he was so late.

So he tol' the lion, if he didn' believe what he had tol' him, to follow him, and he would show him. So, the lion went with the rabbit to the well.

The rabbit tol' the lion to get up on the edge of the well and look down into the well, and he would see what had delayed him. So the lion did. When he looked into the water, he saw the face of another lion, not knowing that it was himself. He frowned, he grit' his teeth, and the other lion did exactly the same thing.

The lion, thinking that he was master of all the beasts of the forest, jumped into the well, and that was the last of the lion. And the rabbit got all the praise of being the wisest beast of the forest.

WHY ARE CATS SO ARROGANT?

Brazil

This is a Brazilian twist on the African folk tale 'The Cat Who Came Indoors' (see the 'Feline Folk Tales of Africa' section, page 15), adapted by storyteller, artist and writer Fabio Sombra from Rio de Janeiro.

Once upon a time, the cat decided that he was born to be the pet of the most powerful animal in the kingdom. All he had to do was find said animal and become their pet.

The cat ventured into the forest and there he found a lion. 'Ah, a lion,' he thought, 'king of the forest. This must be the most powerful animal in the kingdom.' And the cat became the pet of the lion.

Then, one day, an elephant arrived and suddenly the lion appeared to be all scared and subservient, cowering before the elephant. The cat was well and truly disappointed. It appeared the lion wasn't the most powerful animal in the kingdom after all. 'No,' the cat thought, 'it must be the elephant, not the lion, who is the most powerful animal in the kingdom.' And the cat became the pet of the elephant.

Then, one day, a man arrived, and this man carried with him a spear. The elephant took one look at the man with the spear and then fled in fright. The cat, again, was well and truly disappointed. 'I see,' the cat thought to himself, 'the elephant fears man. Man must be the most powerful animal in the kingdom.' And the cat became the pet of the man.

The man brought the cat home and when he arrived, his wife was waiting for him.

'What did you get on today's hunt, what are you bringing? Where is the meat?' the wife asked the man.

'I'm sorry,' said the man, 'but I didn't catch anything today. I was not lucky on my hunt.'

Hearing this, his wife got angry and started yelling at him, so the man rapidly ran away and disappeared out of sight. The cat, puzzled, watched the man run away.

'It looks like I was wrong again,' he thought. 'It seems that man fears woman. Woman is clearly the most powerful animal in the kingdom.' And the cat became the pet of the woman.

Soon afterwards, the woman spotted a mouse on the floor, screamed in terror and leapt up onto a nearby table. The cat quickly got to work, catching the mouse and killing it. 'Wow, if I catch the mouse that scares the most powerful animal in the kingdom, then surely the most powerful of all must be me!' the cat thought to himself with glee.

From that day onwards, the cat was running the risk of becoming the most arrogant animal in the kingdom. Luckily, just as the cat was sitting there contentedly, purring with pride, a dog arrived and chased the cat onto the roof, thus saving it from turning into the most boastfully arrogant of all the species in the kingdom.

CACTUS CAT

Mexico and Southern United States

In my early twenties, I lived in Mexico for a couple of years and even though I didn't hear any tall tales about the Cactus Cat at the time (possibly because my Spanish wasn't anywhere near good enough to grasp such tales), I've become rather partial to this mezcal*-swilling beast that's best disposed of when tipsy. As* mezcal *is made from agave, which isn't a cactus, the nickname is a misnomer, and the Cactus Cats were probably drinking a mixture of fermented cactus sap and* mezcal*. As they say in Oaxaca (home to most of the* mezcal *production),* 'Para todo mal, mezcal, y para todo bien, también; y si no hay remedio, litro y medio' *('For everything bad,* mezcal*, and for everything good, as well; and if there is no remedy, a litre and a half').*

Once upon a time, rumour has it that there were Cactus Cats living throughout the desert area of southwestern United States and throughout Mexico, all the way down to the Yucatán Peninsula on the borders of Belize and Guatemala. Nowadays, this mythical creature is much harder to spot than in the olden days, when it was found roaming more freely, especially at night.

The Cactus Cat is similar to a 'mountain cat' or puma in looks, but it also has thorny or prickly fur and thorns on its ears and tail as protection. Its tail looks like a cactus, with tufts of thorny fur, and it has sharp, bony blades on the forelegs above its front paws. The Cactus Cat uses these foreleg-blades to make deep, slanting slashes at the base of giant cacti and agave plants.

It is said that some of these cats travel in wide circular paths, slashing every single cactus and agave that they see. They time it so that when they return to the start of the first circuit, the sap from the cuts will have fermented into alcohol. The Cactus Cat then lazily laps up the liquid, enjoying the alcoholic brew, and by the time it gets to the end of the second circuit, Cactus Cat is thoroughly drunk and staggers off in a drunken stupor. It makes a very distinctive sound, like a moan or a lament, which, along with the rasping of its bone blades can be heard echoing through the desert at night.

Cactus Cats are said to hollow out large cacti to use as lairs to keep out of the heat and sleep there in daytime, only to roam the desert and countryside at night. They're immune to scorpion venom, feed off insects, and as mentioned, have a great fondness for 'cactus juice' (or should I say, 'cactus booze') and *mezcal*.

This fondness for hard liquor is what became the downfall of the species, as by following a Cactus Cat around, it was easy to collect the *mezcal*, thus depriving the cats of their preferred sustenance. It was hardly an activity without risk, though. *Mezcal* thieves caught in the act were flogged to death by the cat's spiny tail, the red welts looking deceptively like the effects of a severe heat rash. Only when deprived of its source of liquid delight was the otherwise placid Cactus Cat a threat to humans.

THE LYNX WHO ATE HIMSELF

Innu First Nation, Canada

A book of feline folk tales would not be complete without at least one tale about a lynx – a big cat that features in Greek, Norse and North American legends and myths. This rather brutal one, where the Lynx's human wife has the last laugh, is from the Innu First Nation in Newfoundland and Labrador in north-eastern Canada.

There was a lynx who had a habit of marrying and eating Innu women. If he brought nothing home from a hunt, he would attack and eat his wife. One after the other, all his wives mysteriously disappeared. Finally, word got around to the people of the area and in the end, no one would marry Lynx, not even the ugliest and dirtiest of the women.

However, there was one very daring Innu woman, who decided it was time to teach Lynx a lesson.

'I will marry Lynx,' she declared, 'and if he tries anything, I'll kill him before he kills me.'

'Yes, this is worth a try,' said the people, even though they secretly thought she was being reckless to do battle with Lynx, for he was known to be quite a nasty, vicious creature. 'If you think you can kill him, then find him and marry him.'

The woman found Lynx and very soon they were married. All was going well until one day Lynx got back from his hunt empty-handed and hungry.

'Go and fetch some firewood and build a nice roaring fire and I will go fishing to get us some food,' said Lynx to his wife, but she guessed right away what he was up to. No doubt he was planning to throw her onto the fire, roast her and then eat her for dinner.

She did as she was told and gathered plenty of dry firewood, just as Lynx had asked her to. Then she hid herself behind a tree and waited for her husband to return.

Lynx got back, and thinking his wife was in their tent, he repeatedly stabbed it with his spear. All he managed to do was ruin the tent, because his wife was not inside it. He looked for her everywhere – inside the tent, outside the tent – but she was nowhere to be seen. Lynx called to his wife, but no matter how he called out, he received no answer. Finally, in desperation, because Lynx was now very hungry, he decided to eat himself.

'Perhaps I won't taste too bad,' Lynx thought to himself.

And Lynx cut a chunk of meat off his leg, roasted it on the fire and ate it.

'Not bad, not bad at all,' he said to himself. 'I taste rather good.'

Once he'd eaten his entire leg, he continued to roast and eat another leg. Soon he was cutting meat from his entire body, singing as he ate. 'I taste much better than my wives,' he hummed and crooned.

By sunset Lynx had eaten his entire body, there was only his heart left. 'What shall I do?' said Lynx, 'for I am still very hungry.'

Then he thought of something. 'I know what I'll do,' he thought to himself. 'I'll roast my heart and I'll eat it very quickly. That way I'll have a very decent meal before I die.'

All the while, Lynx's wife was watching from behind the tree as her husband tried to quickly roast his own heart on the fire and eat it, but he dropped dead on the spot.

His wife laughed at Lynx's foolishness, then returned to the people. 'I didn't have to kill Lynx,' she told them. 'He killed himself. I didn't have to do a thing.'

EL HOMBRE GATO

Argentina

You might have heard of Catwoman, but what about Catman? This tale from Argentina, El Hombre Gato, *is about just such a creature – the Catman, a male werecat. There are numerous folk tales about werecats from all over the world and they include everything from the domestic moggy (such as witches' familiars) to big cats such as leopards, lions and pumas. Cats as shapeshifters is a common theme in 'catlore'. This is a comparatively modern folk tale, probably originating in the nineteenth century. There are various regional versions from rural parts of Argentina.*

Legend has it that the grassland region of the Pampas, and many other rural areas of Argentina, are home to a creature both fearsome and tantalising, known as *El Hombre Gato*, or the Catman. Rather like a werewolf, this creature is said to be both cat and man – a werecat – and shapeshifts at night. It is hostile and predatory towards humans, hunting them down, tricking and trapping them.

El Hombre Gato usually takes the form of a large, black cat with fiercely glowing eyes. Some say the eyes are bright red and glowing like hot coals, others say they're a menacing yellow or orange. It's a creature of supreme grace and agility, strikingly beautiful, as well as fearsome and terrifying. And this is no ordinary cat – *El Hombre Gato* can easily transform himself into a man.

Where he hails from no one knows, but it is rumoured that this man was once, many moons ago, subjected to a curse uttered by an old witch – a curse that condemned him to wear the skin of an evil, predatory cat. Others claim it is an evil spirit whose physical form is both that of a man and a cat.

A lone *gaucho* was out riding across the pampas one moonlit night when he had a close encounter with *El Hombre Gato*. The *gaucho* spotted a man who seemed to be distressed, and as he was a caring sort, he stopped and got off his horse. Assuming that the man before him was in genuine need of help, he generously offered his assistance, only to find himself led into a trap.

As soon as the *gaucho* had got off his horse to come to the man's aid, the creature revealed his true fearsome features. He transformed into a huge, black feline with terrible glowing eyes and with the speed of lightning, *El Hombre Gato* set upon his rescuer. The *gaucho* escaped by the skin of his teeth, but he was forever haunted by the encounter and the local community lived in fear on moonlit nights for many years to come.

El Hombre Gato's ability to shapeshift is legendary. That's how he can lead his unsuspecting victims astray out on the pampas, it's how he lures them away from safety. He is fast, nimble, fierce and ferocious, he can leap higher and run faster than any other creature. And whatever you do, do not meet his piercing gaze or he might hypnotise you, if you are unlucky enough to look directly into his glaring eyes.

However, despite his supernatural abilities and hunting prowess even *El Hombre Gato* is not invincible. Rumour has it that silver objects, especially weapons, can cause harm to the much-feared were-cat and it's also possible to stop him from transforming back into a man if captured in his feline form. But if you find yourself out on the pampas on a moonlit night, beware and be cautious. *El Hombre Gato* has never been captured and few are those who have seen him and lived to tell the tale.

He might be out there, waiting for you.

WAIT UNTIL EMMETT COMES

United States

This is a rather spooky story thought to be of African-American origin, from the Southern states or West Virginia, with early versions dating back to the 1700s. The story evolved through the 1700 and 1800s, and there are multiple versions. The one included here was retold to me by UK-based storyteller Amelia Ace Armande, from Ropetackle Storytellers.

Late one December evening, a lone preacher was out riding on his way to one of the churches under his care. It was a very dark night and a storm was a-comin'. There was only one house within reach, an old mansion that was known to be haunted. The wind got up, the rain came down and the preacherman had no choice, but to seek shelter from the storm. Clutching his Bible in one hand, he headed straight for the mansion, saying to himself, 'The Good Lawd will look after me and keep me safe'.

The preacherman reached the mansion just as the fierce storm was breaking. Once he'd taken his horse to a nearby barn, he swiftly made his way to the large manor house itself. Much to his surprise, he found that the door was unlocked. He went through the hallway and into a large room where a huge fireplace was covering an entire wall in the room. By a stroke of luck, the fireplace was piled high with wood, just waiting to be lit and as it was a cold December night, he didn't hesitate but struck a match and lit the fire. As a good blaze got going, the preacher quietly sat down to warm up and read his Bible in the light from the fire.

All was eerie and ghostly, inside there was just the gentle sound of the fire crackling, while the storm was howling outside. Slowly, the fire burnt right down to a glowing heap of coals and the storm continued unabated.

Suddenly, the preacherman stopped reading, startled by an unexpected sound quite nearby. Looking up from his Bible, he saw the strangest of sights. Right there, a very large, black cat was leisurely stretching as cats often do, before walking up to the fireplace and sitting itself down amongst the red-hot coals. As the preacher watched, mesmerised, the cat took a coal in its paw and began to lick it ever so slowly. Then it got up, shook the ashes off its fur, and walked right up to where the preacher was sitting. Its fierce yellow eyes gazed upon him, its black tail was thumping against the floorboards, and then the cat spoke.

'Wait until Emmett comes', it said, quietly.

The preacherman nearly dropped the Bible in shock and skipped right into the New Testament. Never before had he heard of a cat talking. He kept on reading his Bible, feeling ever so nervous and muttering to himself, 'The Good Lawd will look after me and keep me safe.'

Not long afterwards, another cat arrived. This one was as black as midnight, and the preacher had never seen such a large cat before – it was as large as the largest of dogs. This cat too lay down amongst the red-hot coals, pouncing at them with enormous paws. Finally, it walked over to the other cat.

'What shall we do with him?' the large cat asked.

'We shouldn't do nothin'. We should wait until Emmett comes,' replied the other.

Both cats, black as midnight, now just sat there watching the preacher, who was reading through the Gospels in a nervous frenzy, aware as he was of the two pairs of fearsome yellow eyes staring at him.

Then, just as the preacher's tension was reaching fever pitch, a third cat, the size of a tiger, entered the room. This cat too went to the fireplace full of red-hot coals and rolled among them, even biting and chewing at them before spitting them out again with a hiss. The tiger-cat then joined the other two, facing the preacher in his chair.

'What shall we do with him?' it practically growled to the others.

'We shouldn't do nothin'. We should wait until Emmett comes,' the other cats replied as one.

The preacherman had by now reached the Book of Revelation and, looking furtively around the room, he closed his Bible and he stood up. 'Goo'night cats, I thank you for your company. When Emmett comes, you tell him I been here and I been gone,' said the preacherman and off he went into the night as swiftly as though he had the Devil himself following hot on his tail.

THE CAT, THE DOG AND DEATH

Haiti

It's surprisingly rare for God to feature in a folk tale (the same goes for Jesus, the angels and biblical characters in general), while the Devil and demons in all their guises crop up with monotonous regularity. In this explanatory tale from Haiti, however, God takes centre stage when a cat and a dog set out to visit his abode and make their opinions on eternal life known to him. The cat has a lot to answer for …

In ancient times, in the beginning of things, God had not yet made up his mind about whether the creatures he had created should live forever. The question had not yet been decided. The cat and the dog decided to sit down together and have a discussion on the subject.

'It is my opinion that when creatures have lived their lives, they should not go on living forever,' said the cat.

'Oh no, on the contrary – I think that we should live for all time,' the dog countered.

'No, no one should live forever,' the cat insisted. 'When one has lived one's life, that truly is enough.'

'I shall go and see God about this matter,' said the dog 'and I shall insist that all creatures should live forever.'

'I too will go and see God about this question of great importance,' the cat similarly declared, 'for I firmly believe that they should not.'

Thus, they parted ways.

The dog wondered what he might do to delay the cat. He took some butter, placed it on a banana leaf and placed said leaf near the path where the cat could not fail to spot it. The cat, of course, was no different and he too considered carefully what he might do to delay the dog. He found a large, juicy bone and he placed it near the path, where the dog couldn't fail to spot it. Then the cat returned home and groomed and dressed himself before beginning his journey to God. The dog too got himself clean and dressed before beginning his own journey to God's abode. And so, they were both ready and set off towards God's house.

When the cat came to the place where the dog had placed the butter, he simply ignored it and continued on his way. When the dog came to the place where the cat had placed the juicy bone, he could smell it. He stopped to have a sniff, but then said to himself, 'This is no time to be stopping'.

Just as he was passing the bone, his head turned so that his nose was pointing right at it. This time the dog stopped and sat down. 'This is no time to be pointing,' he said to his nose.

Again, he started to move along the path, but his head turned further and further, until finally the dog's nose was pointing backwards, towards his tail. That's when the dog turned back and started gnawing on the juicy bone that the cat had so cleverly left near the path to distract him from his true mission.

Meanwhile, the cat was now arriving at God's house.

'What is it that you are here to tell me?' God asked the cat.

'I have come to tell you that when a person has lived out his life, he should live no longer,' the cat answered.

God thought about this statement for quite some time and then at last he turned to the cat. 'Very well,' God said, 'so it shall be.'

When the dog at long last finished gnawing the bone, he too continued on his way and reached God's house.

'What is it that you are here to tell me?' God asked the dog.

'I have come to tell you that all creatures should live forever,' the dog answered.

'You are too late,' God proclaimed, 'the decision has already been made.'

And so it is that no creature lives forever. Because dog could not resist the juicy bone, he was too late and did not arrive in time. And so it is with dogs to this day – they cannot pass a bone anywhere without giving it a great deal of attention.

WHY DOGS CHASE CATS

United States

An African-American folk tale explaining how dogs and cats have traditionally come to be seen as such sworn enemies. There are many takes on this tale from different parts of the world, for example China (see Australasia section, page 55). In most cases, cats and dogs start off as friends, or as in this tale, as a married couple, before things take a different turn.

A long, long time ago, Dog and Cat were living as a married couple, sharing the same home, and not only were they married, but they were very happy together, living in harmony. But then something changed …

Every night, when Dog returned home from work completely exhausted and worn out, Cat told him that she was not feeling very well. The fact was, she was too sick to make them dinner. Well now, Dog, he was a patient sort of creature and, on the whole, very caring and understanding, but this same pattern repeated itself over and over again. Every night when Dog got back home after his working day, Cat proclaimed that she was sadly way too sick to cook them dinner.

Dog believed Cat and was truly sorry that she felt so unwell day after day, poor kitty. As the days went by, however, Dog got more and more fed up with fixing dinner for the pair of them after a hard day's work. Cat, after all, just stayed at home all day long, resting up, but no matter how she rested she never seem to be getting any better.

The longer this went on for, the more fed up and unhappy Dog was getting. Finally, one day, he'd had enough. He simply told Cat that he was off to work as usual that morning, but he was sneaky and instead of setting off for work he hid in a large cupboard to spy on Cat. He wanted to see for himself if Cat really was as sick as she claimed to be.

Dream of Dog's surprise when, not a minute after Cat thought he'd left for work, she started playing games with Kitten. The pair of them were running about and frolicking, jumping and pouncing and having the best of times. Cat, as it turned out, wasn't in the least bit sick. Instead, she was just enjoying herself day after day, together with Kitten. Fit as a fiddle, she was, leaping about.

Dog, sitting quietly in his hiding place, became filled with rage at the injustice of it all. He sat there fuming and furious, thinking about all those damn dinners he'd been made to cook for himself and Cat night after night. He leapt out of the cupboard, barking and growling, making a fearsome racket.

As soon as Cat saw him, she swiftly stuck a marble in her cheek. Thinking on her feet, the cunning kitty claimed she had a toothache. Dog was having none of it, he refused to be fooled again. Would you believe he was so mad that he started chasing Cat all around the house. Round and round they went as fast as they could, with Dog barking ferociously and Cat hissing fiercely.

From that day onwards, Dogs always chase Cats.

THE CAT'S LEAP

Brazil

This Brazilian folk tale, which is pitting big cat against small cat, imaginatively explains how one of the country's best-known sayings came about. 'The cat's leap' or 'o pulo do gato', *means to have something up your sleeve, a 'pièce de resistance trick'. The moral of the story? Not to give away your best trick, but always keep something back, like this clever – and ever so agile – kitty.*

It is a well-known fact that a jaguar is very agile and has many useful skills. The jaguar in this tale, however, was in fact very envious of the domestic cat. He thought cats were even more skilled and knew far more tricks than he did himself. Cats always landed on their feet, for example, and that was just one of the many tricks the jaguar thought he could benefit from learning.

He waited for the right opportunity and then asked the local neighbourhood cat if she could teach him some of her tricks. In exchange, the jaguar would bring the cat an ample supply of the prey he caught, so that the cat would always have something to eat. The cat deliberated for some time before she responded.

'Very well, this set-up works for me,' she said at last. 'I will teach you my skills and every day you will bring me some of the prey you catch.'

And so the cat began teaching the jaguar all the tricks she knew, making the jaguar a more agile, swift and cunning hunter than ever before, while the jaguar regularly brought fresh meat or freshly caught fish to the cat.

A good few weeks passed and the cat carried on with the lessons as agreed, even teaching the jaguar the supremely difficult double-twisted jump, which in time he mastered, despite his heavier bulk. You see, this jaguar was quite a fast learner, and he had a secret incentive to get to the end of the lessons as quickly as he could. All in all, he found his time in training with the cat to be very useful indeed.

The jaguar reached the end of his training and the day of the very last lesson arrived. At the end of it, the jaguar, who was not to be trusted, thought to himself, 'Right, now that I know all the cat's tricks, it's time to test my skills even further. I will catch this kitty and I will eat her.'

After the lesson, the jaguar thanked the cat profusely for all that she'd taught him, then they said their goodbyes and turned to go their separate ways – or so the cat thought. When the cat had her back to the jaguar, he unexpectedly lunged at her.

Much to the jaguar's astonishment, however, the cat leapt up into a nearby tree, using a technique of such splendid agility that she easily escaped the jaguar's gaping jaws and fearsome teeth. The jaguar sat staring after the cat in stunned silence, mightily annoyed. 'Hey kitty!' he hollered after her. 'You didn't teach me that trick!'

'No, I did not,' the cat answered with a hiss and a growl, 'and I never will. That leap is what I call 'the cat's leap', '*o pulo do gato*'. What's more, here's a life lesson for you and the last thing I'll ever teach you – poor is the master who teaches his students all his tricks.'

THREE WISHES

United States

A wonderfully humorous tale of 'be careful what you wish for', in case you get it. Or almost get it, as it were. There are numerous versions of this story. In one, the old lady is depicted as Cinderella after her prince has passed on to the afterlife and she's living alone with her cat.

Once there was a very old woman, so old in fact that she was by now both toothless and thin-haired, wrinkly and weak-eyed. She was living all by herself in a quaint little cottage together with her loyal male cat, who had been with her for many years. The old woman and her cat were both sitting, dozing, by the open fire late one night, when out of the blue an elf suddenly appeared as if by magic.

The old woman was mightily startled by this strange creature, appearing without warning. She nearly jumped out of her skin, despite the state of her weary old bones and she quite sent the cat flying off her lap when she moved. Well, it's not every day that an elf pays you a visit, of course, so this woman swiftly snapped out of her stupor and roused herself.

'Who might you be then? And what might you want at this late hour?' she asked, a tad suspicious.

'I am here to grant you three wishes,' the elf responded, taking off his hat and giving her an ever so toothy grin.

'Three wishes, you say. Is that so?'

The old woman remained suspicious at first, but the elf assured her that there were no catches, no tricks and nothing to be suspicious of at all. She'd had such a long, hard life, he said, and he felt she deserved to be rewarded for all her troubles and travails. Make no mistake, he really *had* arrived to grant her three wishes and begged her to please tell him what her wishes would be.

'I don't believe you. No, surely it's all a hoax,' said the old woman.

'No, no, dear mistress, it is all true,' the elf countered.

This to-ing and fro-ing went on for quite some time, but at long last, the old woman was convinced and began to ponder her wishes in earnest. She even got up and paced the room to get the little grey cells in motion.

Then she smiled and turned to the elf. 'Right,' she said, 'I've thought about it and these are my three wishes. First of all, I wish I were fabulously rich and wealthy. Second, I wish I were young and very beautiful again.'

Then she stopped. What about the third wish? She pondered and she racked her brains, until – aha! – she'd got it.

'See this cat right here? Well, as my third and last wish, I wish that my loyal cat would turn into the most handsome, the most attractive, the sexiest young man you could imagine.'

'Your wishes will be granted,' the elf solemnly declared and without another word he disappeared.

The woman noticed nothing different after the elf's departure. She sat there and waited and waited but much to her disappointment, nothing happened. 'I knew it,' she said bitterly, 'I knew it was a hoax.'

Soon she was fast asleep by the open fire again – she was very old after all. When she woke up a few hours later, she immediately sensed that something was different. She opened her eyes and looked around, and lo and behold, her house was as elegant as anything, ornate and richly furnished, she must be very rich indeed. She positively sprinted to the nearest mirror and, yes, looking in the mirror, she found that she was at least seventy years younger than before and exceedingly beautiful, just like the elf had promised. Remembering her third wish, she then dashed back to the room with the open fire and there, on the couch, was the most attractive young man she had ever seen in her entire life. She sat down beside him and he put his arms around her, looked her deep in the eyes and said, 'Now aren't you sorry you had me fixed all those years ago?'

FELINE FOLK TALES OF AUSTRALASIA

When researching folk tales from Australia, New Zealand and the Pacific Islands, I hit a snag for obvious reasons – namely that cats, domestic and feral, are comparatively new to the region, having been brought over by European colonisers in 1788 onboard the First Fleet: eleven British ships with convicts, soldiers and, one would imagine, a healthy number of ships' cats (see also the 'Superstitions, Sayings and Ships' Cats' chapter, page 165). As folk tales tend to evolve over time, sometimes over several centuries, it's not surprising that there are few feline folk tales from this part of the world.

However, they do exist; an overview of Australian cat tales is included in this chapter. For the most part, these tales date from the last fifty years or so and arguably fall under the headline 'urban myth' rather than folk tale. Not focusing on your average domestic moggie, several of the tales retell sightings of ghostly big cats, such as the Blue Mountains panther.

This lack of kitty tales is amply made up for by Asia, where you're spoilt for choice. Japan stands out as a nation of cat lovers and Japanese folk tales featuring every aspect of the cat deserve a book of their own. No less than five Japanese tales are included here. Other nations tell cat tales too and you'll find tales from China, Korea, the Middle East, Tibet, Malaysia, India, Taiwan and the Philippines. While Japan favours domestic cats, tigers, lions and panthers feature in some of the other feline folk tales in this section.

THE TALE OF MUEZZA, THE PROPHET MUHAMMAD'S CAT

Middle East

Over the years, I have come across several versions of this rather sweet tale, which depicts the Prophet Muhammad as a firm felinophile. On a personal note, it reminds me of the many beautiful felines I saw around the mosques of Marrakesh on a visit to Morocco (and also goes some way towards explaining the cats' constant presence near mosques).

As the call to prayer sounded at sunset, the Prophet Muhammad was preparing to go to the mosque. He went to put on his robe, but there, peacefully sleeping on one of the sleeves, was a small stray cat. The prophet hesitated and paused, wondering what to do. He did not wish to disturb the kitten's quiet slumber. Instead of waking and moving the cat, he ever so gently cut off the section of his sleeve where the kitten lay snoozing and got dressed for prayer without having to rouse the sleeping feline.

When the prophet returned from prayer, the kitten awoke naturally and soon began rubbing herself affectionately against his leg as a thank you for letting her sleep in peace. He smiled, picking up the sweet and loving kitty, bringing her with him into his own house. Once home, he gave her some food to eat and fresh water to drink and let her make herself comfortable on his lap. From that day onwards, this cat became known as Muezza, the Prophet Muhammad's own beloved cat companion.

The prophet's followers were surprised by such kindness shown to a mere stray cat. Why, they asked, did he care so much about such a lowly creature when surely, he had far more important matters to take care of? But the Prophet Muhammad turned to his followers and said, 'To show mercy, no matter how small, is a good deed. How can you be so unfeeling as to not care for the weak? This cat deserves every bit as much compassion as any human being.'

From that day onwards, the prophet made sure that all the stray cats that could be found living in or near his mosque were always well looked after, fed and sheltered. His disciples were told to follow his example in treating all animals well. Newborn kittens were taken care of and always found caring homes. The Prophet Muhammad thought of caring for cats, and other animals, as part of living a moral life.

Finding Muezza asleep on his sleeve is seen as a moment that shaped the Prophet Muhammad's enduring legacy of compassion. Those who mistreated felines were warned that 'Acts of cruelty towards animals are as harmful as those towards humans'. Cats were welcome to come to rest or dwell in his mosque without fear of being chased or harassed. And as for Muezza, she remained a familiar, purring presence, always comfortable on the Prophet Muhammad's lap while he spent his days teaching.

THE LION AND THE HARE

The Panchatantra *Books, India*

This is quite possibly the original version of the tale of the hare outsmarting the lion, from the Panchatantra *books from India. Similar stories, albeit with different animals, can be found across the globe and several are included in this book (see 'Lion Brooks No Rival' in the Americas section, page 34, 'Old Mountain Uncle' and 'The Tiger and the Shadow', later in this section, pages 89 and 99).*

In the middle of a forest there lived a lion who was known as Bhâsuraka, or 'Heroic One'. His great strength meant that he was unceasingly killing gazelles, hares and many other animals.

One day, all the creatures of the forest gathered together. Gazelles, boars, buffalo, wild oxen, hares and so forth, went to see the lion.

'Sir, why are you unnecessarily murdering all the wild animals, when one animal would be sufficient to fill you up?' they asked him. 'We urge you to enter into an agreement with us. From this day onwards, you may sit here quietly and wait. Every day, when it's his turn, one animal will come to you and allow you to eat him. In this manner, you can acquire all your nourishment without effort and thus we won't be exterminated. That is the right of a king and let it thus be carried out.'

Bhâsuraka listened carefully to their words and then spoke. 'What you say is true,' he agreed, 'but if ever an animal fails to come to me here, then I promise you, I will surely devour you all.'

They sealed their promise with the words 'So it shall be', and now, free of danger, all the animals were able to move fearlessly about the forest. Each and every day, in turn, an animal went to the lion: an old one; one who had renounced all earthly affairs; one who was torn by grief; as well as one who feared he might lose his wife and children. Every day at noon, one animal presented himself to the lion to serve as his meal.

Following a predetermined order, it soon became the hare's turn, and however little he liked it, he was sent to the lion by the other animals. He walked as slowly as possible and thus missed the established deadline of midday. With fear in his heart, the hare sought a way to escape death. Finally, towards the end of the day he reached the lion. Famished from his long wait, the lion was filled with rage. Licking the corners of his mouth, he was already plotting his revenge. 'Tomorrow I shall kill all the creatures in the forest,' he thought.

Just as he was thinking this, along came the hare, walking right up to the lion and, bowing, stood before him. When the lion saw that it was the hare, who was usually so light-footed, who was the one who had arrived so late, he became even angrier. 'Hey you, miserable little hare,' he growled. 'So it had to be you, arriving so long after the appointed time, you who is the most light-footed of them all. Because of your failure to keep to the appointed time, tomorrow I am going to exterminate all the rest of the animals, after I've devoured you.'

On hearing this, the hare bowed deeply and reverently to the lion. 'Sir, it is neither my fault nor the fault of the other animals. Would you like to hear the cause of my tardiness?' the hare asked humbly.

'Speak quickly, before you find yourself between my teeth!' the lion roared at him.

'Sir, please listen,' said the hare. 'After learning from the other animals that today was my turn, I was sent away together with four hares. On my way here I was approached by another large lion, who came out from his lair and said to me, "Hey there, where are you going? Pay homage to your guardian angel." I told him that we were on our way to our lord Bhâsuraka, to keep our contract with him and serve as his meal. To this, the other lion said, "If that is so, then all of the animals must also enter into a contract with me, because this forest belongs to me. This Bhâsuraka you speak of sounds just like a miserable little thief to me, but if he really is king here, then I demand you leave the four hares here as hostages and that he come here at once, so that the one of us who can prove himself king through his strength will be able to eat all the animals here." Following this other lion's orders, I came here and that is the reason why I am late. Now your order is my command, good Sir.'

Upon hearing this, Bhâsuraka said, 'If this is the case, then quickly show me this rogue of a lion so I can vent my anger against the other animals on him and become myself once again.'

'Sir, you are right,' said the hare. 'We warriors go to battle to protect our homeland and to fight against evil. This enemy lives in a castle. If he attacks us from his castle, we'll be threatened, but if he stays in his castle, he'll be difficult to overcome.'

'Lead me to this rogue,' Bhâsuraka continued. 'Even if he is in a castle, I will kill him.'

'Wait,' said the hare. 'I have seen that he is very powerful. Sir, it is not good for you to go without knowing his strength.'

'Bah! What is it to you?' Bhâsuraka insisted. 'Lead me to him, even if he does live in a castle.'

'Well, if you insist,' said the hare, 'come with me, sir.'

They both set off together and when they got to a well, the hare stopped. There he said to Bhâsuraka, 'Sir, who is able to withstand your majesty? This rogue saw you coming from afar and has retreated into his castle. Come here and I will show him to you.'

Upon hearing this, Bhâsuraka said, 'Show me his castle at once!'

Then the hare showed him the well. The foolish lion, seeing his own reflection in the middle of the well, roared fiercely. A doubly loud roar echoed up from within the well.

Hearing this, he thought, 'He is indeed very powerful', and he threw himself upon him, and thus he lost his life.

The hare, on the other hand, after having cheerfully reported back to the other animals, was greatly praised by them, and he lived happily in the forest all of his days.

WHY DOGS WAG THEIR TAILS

The Philippines

One of many folk tales explaining not only why cats and dogs are enemies (see also, for example, 'Why Dogs and Cats are Enemies', later in this section on page 77 and 'Why Dogs Chase Cats', in the Americas section, page 48), but why dogs wag their tails and why cats avoid water. It is the only tale in this collection featuring a dog, but no cat, in the story title!

A rich man in a certain town once owned a dog and a cat, and they were of great use to him. The dog had served his master faithfully for such a long time, and had become so old that he had lost all his teeth and was unable to fight any more. The dog was a good guide and companion to the cat, who was still strong and also cunning.

The master had a daughter, who was attending school at a convent some distance away from home, and from time to time he would send the dog and the cat to take presents to the girl. One day, he called the faithful animals over to his side and requested that they carry a magic ring to his daughter. 'You are strong and you are courageous,' he said to the cat. 'You may carry this magic ring, but you must be very careful not to drop it,' while to the dog, he said, 'You must accompany the cat to guide her and keep her out of harm's way.'

The two of them promised to do their best and so they started out together. All was going well, but then they suddenly reached a wide river. As there was neither bridge nor boat for the stalwart pair to use, there was nothing for it, they would need to swim to get across.

'Let me carry the magic ring,' said the dog as they were about to enter the water and make their way to the other side.

'Oh, no,' the cat replied, 'master gave it to me to carry and it is up to me to take it safely across.'

'But you cannot swim very well,' the dog argued. 'I am a much stronger swimmer, and you can trust me to take good care of it.'

The cat stood her ground and refused to give up the ring. It wasn't until the dog got fierce and threatened to kill her if she didn't hand it over that she finally, reluctantly, passed it to him to carry across the waters. The river was wide, and the water was so fast-flowing that they both grew increasingly tired and just before they reached the opposite bank the dog accidentally dropped the precious magic ring. No matter how carefully they searched for it, they could not find it anywhere and so they had to return home to tell their master of the sad loss.

Before they even reached the house, however, the dog, who wasn't as brave as the cat, became so fearful that he abruptly turned around, ran away, and from that day onwards was never seen again. The brave cat carried on towards home, ready to face the master all alone.

When he saw her coming, he immediately wanted to know why she was back so soon and what had become of her companion. The poor cat was very scared, but she explained as best she could what had happened, how the ring had been lost and how the dog had run away. Upon hearing this story, the master became so enraged that he sent out all his people in search of the dog, with strict instructions to cut off the dog's tail as punishment for losing the ring and running away. The master also ordered that all the dogs in the world should join in the search.

Ever since, when one dog meets another, he asks, 'Are you the old dog that lost the magic ring? If so, your tail must be cut off.' Immediately, each dog will then show his teeth and wag his tail to prove that he is not the guilty one. And ever since that day, cats have been afraid of water and will never swim across a river if they can avoid it.

MANEKI-NEKO, THE BECKONING CAT

Japan

Who hasn't spotted the beckoning cat, with its waving paw, on display in numerous shop and restaurant windows, on counters and many other places? Here's the tale of how the Maneki-neko, *the Beckoning Cat from Japan, became a symbol of good luck. There are various versions of this story, including one where the* Maneki-neko *saves a man from a lightning strike by beckoning him to cross the street.*

A long, long time ago, a boy named Yohei lived with his father in a small village by the sea. Every morning, as the sun rose out of the ocean, Yohei got up and went down to the port to buy fish. Then he went door-to-door, selling the fish he'd bought fresh from the fishermen. He carried the fish in two wooden baskets, dangling from a pole that he balanced across his shoulders.

Despite Yohei working very hard, he remained very poor. Then, as fate would have it, his father sadly fell ill. Yohei began working even harder to try to make more money so that he could buy his father some medicine to get better. But the poor boy was only able to carry two baskets of fish at any one time. Oh, how he wished and hoped that he would be able to sell more than he could carry. One rainy evening, as Yohei was cooking rice at home, he suddenly became aware of a tap at his door. When he opened it, right on his doorstep he saw a cat, sitting there, sodden and shivering in the driving rain. Her white fur was covered in mud and she meowed plaintively, begging to be let into the house.

'Oh, you poor little stray kitty,' Yohei said and he opened the door wider, inviting her in. Once inside, he gently dried her off with a soft towel.

After giving his father his supper, Yohei took some rice and half the fish from the paltry offerings on his own plate and gave them to the stray cat. The cat finished eating the yummy fish and then promptly jumped onto Yohei's lap, rubbing her soft, white fur against her rescuer. Although Yohei went hungry that night, the cat's soft purring made him feel happy that he'd given her some food, nonetheless. The very next morning, however, Yohei found that the cat had disappeared.

Three days went by and Yohei was out selling fish in the village when his neighbour, Masa, came running towards him, crying out to him, 'Come! You must come quickly – your father is running a high fever.' Yohei set off for home in flash, still carrying the baskets heavy with fresh fish. When he returned home, much to his surprise, there was the cat again, waiting by the door. Yohei was in such a hurry to see his father that he didn't even give himself time to stop. He rushed into his father's room, placed a cool, damp cloth on his forehead and made sure he was as comfortable as possible.

Then he looked at all the fresh fish and sighed. 'What shall I do?' Yohei thought to himself. 'I can't leave my father to go and sell the fish today and by tomorrow it will have spoiled.'

Just as he was wringing his hands in despair, there was a knock at the door. When Yohei went to answer, he saw a young woman in a multicoloured silk kimono standing before him.

'Hello, how may I help you?' Yohei asked, very surprised to see her.

'Do you sell fish?' the young woman asked, pointing to the baskets full of fresh fish. 'How funny, a cat calling a customer to a fishmonger!' she continued, laughing now.

'What do you mean?' Yohei asked her.

'Isn't she your cat? The white one. After I left my teacher's home, she came and meowed at me and waved her paw as if to say, "Come here". She was so adorable that I followed her.'

Yohei was astonished. He told the young woman about the cat's first visit to him.

'What a remarkable kitty,' the young woman commented. 'She must have beckoned to me to come and buy your fish.' She asked Yohei to wrap up three fish for her.

Bowing, Yohei thanked her, and she left.

Soon afterwards, there was another knock at the door and when he answered it, Yohei saw the owner of a large store in a nearby town, an elderly man.

'Hello, good sir, what brings you here?' Yohei asked, even more surprised to see such a rich merchant visiting his humble abode.

'Ah, so it was your cat,' said the merchant, his eyes widening in surprise. 'She must have heard me talking about fish.'

'About fish?' Yohei said, more puzzled by the minute.

'Yes, about fish. You see, this morning, my daughter-in-law gave birth to a baby boy and I wanted ten large red snappers for the party I'm giving in honour of my grandson. I left home in search of a fishmonger. Then your white cat found me, started meowing and beckoning to me with her paw.' At this, the merchant began waving his hand, mimicking the cat's gesture. 'I couldn't help but follow her and here you are with all this fish.'

Yohei was so mightily surprised that he told the merchant everything about his father and the cat's arrival at their home.

'My goodness, she is gathering customers on your behalf,' the merchant said. 'I have never heard of a cat repaying a kindness in such a way. These days even people forget to show their gratitude.' The merchant extracted a silver coin large enough to buy a whole basket of fish and proceeded to hand it over to Yohei.

'This is the money for the snappers. Keep the change and look after your father.'

Yohei thanked the merchant profusely with deep bows.

One after another, people came to Yohei's home that day, beckoned by the cat. By the afternoon, both baskets of fish were empty. All the customers praised the cat and promised to come back the next day and, in this way, Yohei was able to sell his fish, while also looking after his father.

And from that day onwards, the little white cat lived with Yohei and kept inviting customers. Some came from far away just to see the beckoning cat. Yohei, meanwhile, was able to sell more and more fish and soon he could open his very own shop. His father recovered, thanks to the medicine Yohei was able to procure.

The other merchants wished they too had a cat as clever Yohei's, and this is how the beckoning cat turned into a symbol of good luck and fortune. Throughout Japan, people began making porcelain cats holding up and waving one paw, just like Yohei's cat. Merchants and businesses of all kinds began putting them in their stores, hoping to attract new customers and welcome old ones. If you see the *Maneki-neko*, the Beckoning Cat, in windows or on counters, now you know why.

THE CAT AS HOLY MAN

Palestine

Another tale of a devious and cunning cat, this one from Palestine with, unusually for a feline folk tale, a religious twist. In this tale, at least, the mice are not taken in by the cat's 'conversion'.

A town cat, having devoured almost all the mice and rats in its surroundings, found himself forced, for lack of prey, to go into the fields and hunt for birds, mice, rats and lizards. Times were tough and so the cat thought of the following ruse.

Keeping away from his usual haunts for several weeks, he returned and lay down in front of a mouse and rat warren with a rosary round his neck. Then, eyes closed, he began to purr loudly and sonorously. Soon a mouse peeped out of a hole, but seeing the cat, hastily retreated.

'Why do you run away,' said the pussycat gently, 'instead of showing pleasure at an old neighbour returning from pilgrimage? You run away as soon as you see him. Come and visit me, you have nothing fear.'

Surprised at hearing himself thus addressed, the mouse tentatively ventured to the opening of his hole again. 'How can you expect me to visit you?' the mouse countered. 'Are you not the enemy of my race? Should I accept your invitation, you would surely seize and devour me as you did with my parents and so many others of my kindred mice.'

'Alas,' sighed the cat, 'your reproaches are just and true, for I have been a great sinner and have earned this abuse and enmity. But rest assured that I am truly penitent and reformed. As you can see from this rosary round my neck, I now devote myself to prayer, meditation and the recital of holy books, the whole of which I have learnt by heart. I was just beginning to recite when you happened to look out of your hole. Not only that, but I have visited the Holy Places, so am a *Hajji* as well as a *Hâfiz*. Go, my injured but nevertheless generous and forgiving friend, and make my change of life and sentiments known to the rest of your kin. Please bid them no longer shun my society, seeing that I am become a recluse. Whilst you are absent, I shall resume my recitations. *Purr, purr, purr.*'

Surprised and astonished at the news he had just heard, the mouse made the cat's statements known to the rest of the tribe. At first, they were incredulous, but as one after another had ventured to peep out from their holes to behold the whiskered ascetic with the rosary round his neck, apparently oblivious to all earthly concerns, steadily repeating his *purr, purr, purr*, which they could only suppose to be the contents of holy books, they came to the conclusion that there might be some truth in the matter, and they convened a meeting of mice and rats to discuss how to proceed.

After much heated debate, it was judged to be only right that they test the veracity of the cat's conversion, but they agreed to be prudent at the same time; and so, a large and experienced rat was sent out on a recce. This wary veteran kept well out of the cat's reach, although he saluted him respectfully and politely from a safe distance.

The cat allowed the rat to prowl about unmolested for quite some time in the hope that other rats and mice would come out, thus allowing him easy access to plenty of prey. The mice and the rats did not come, however, and at long last the pangs of hunger overcame the 'holy cat.' He could wait no longer and got ready to pounce.

The rat, however, was on high alert for signs of danger and darted off the instant he noticed, from a slight movement of the cat's muscles, that the pretended saint was about to kill him.

'Why do you dash away so abruptly?' mewed the cat. 'Surely you are not tired of hearing me repeat the scriptures, or do you doubt the correctness of my recitation?'

'Neither I trust,' answered the rat as he peeped out from the hole in which he had taken refuge. 'I am convinced that, however much you may have learnt by rote, you have neither unlearnt nor eschewed your habits of pouncing upon us poor mice.'

HÓO-KOO-PÔ, THE TIGER AUNT

Taiwan

There are many folk tales from around the world that contain a cautionary element, whether aimed at children or adults. Here's a beware-of-strangers tale from Taiwan, aimed at children. The stranger is in this case known as 'tiger aunt', 'tiger grandmother' or in some versions, 'tiger witch' (there are several hundred versions from across Taiwan). This is arguably a story about a spirit, not a cat, so I'm stretching the big cat definition by including it as a feline folk tale, but I felt it merited inclusion for its tiger title. It's reminiscent of 'Little Red Riding Hood', 'Hansel and Gretel' and other cautionary children's tales. China, Japan and Korea all have their own versions.

Once upon a time, there were two young sisters, living with their loving parents in a remote part of Taiwan. As it happened, the parents had to set off on a trip to the city one day and be away for a couple of days. They left careful instructions for their two children to look after the house and, above all, not to open the door to strangers.

'No problem at all,' the sisters replied in unison, happily waving goodbye to their parents as they were leaving the little house.

What the two sisters didn't know, however, was that nearby, hiding in the bushes, was the ancient spirit of a tigress, watching, waiting and biding her time. After thousands of years of hard training, this ancient spirit had turned into an evil tiger witch. And this tiger witch – well, she specialised in eating children!

The tiger witch stayed hidden, watching and waiting until there was no more sign of the parents. Then she sneaked out of her hiding place and went over to knock on the sisters' door. To be extra certain they would let her in, she came prepared with plenty of sweets and sugary treats.

The girls tentatively opened the door and saw a strange creature standing there on the doorstep. 'Who are you?' the girls asked the tiger witch.

'I'm your great-aunt – your tiger aunt,' came the reply. 'And before they left, your parents asked me to come and stay here with you while they're away from home. Look, I've brought you some candy and other yummy treats.'

Of course, seeing such an abundance of their favourite sweets made the girls drop their guard completely, forgetting all about not opening the door to strangers, and they soon invited their 'tiger aunt' into the house.

Tiger aunt was cunning and readily reassured the two sisters that she would help keep them safe while their parents were away.

'Don't worry, my dears, I will stay with you all night,' she promised, 'to make sure you won't be afraid of the dark. You'll come to no harm as long as you stay close to me.'

In the middle of the night, the oldest of the two girls suddenly woke up quite by accident. She opened her eyes just in time to see that the tiger aunt was busy devouring her little sister in one swift mouthful. The older sister fought against her terror with all her might, trying not to scream. Slowly, she managed to calm herself down and made herself pretend that she hadn't noticed that her little sister had disappeared. She got up, turned to the tiger aunt and asked if she could go to the outhouse. As soon as she made it outside, the older sister climbed as high up a tree as she could manage, keeping well out of the reach of the tiger aunt. Some time went by, and tiger aunt waited, ready for her next meal, but the girl didn't return.

Finally, the wicked tiger witch went out to look for her. As soon as she realised she'd been tricked, she became livid. The older girl had managed to escape up a tree and tiger aunt furiously demanded that she climb back down this instant.

'Well,' the young girl was weighing her words carefully, 'I will certainly come down, but before I do, I think you ought to prepare some peanut oil to season me with, that way I will taste so much better when you eat me.'

The tiger aunt thought this was solid advice and immediately began heating up a large pot of peanut oil. As soon as the tiger aunt had heated the peanut oil, the oldest sister suggested bringing the pot of oil up the tree with a rope so that she could season herself with the oil. The tiger aunt thought the girl was being nicely obliging and sent the pot up the tree as requested. When the clever girl got the pot, she immediately tipped its boiling contents all over the tiger aunt, who was waiting for her next meal right beneath the tree.

Evil tiger aunt died instantly, burnt to death by the hot peanut oil. And so, even though the girl had lost her younger sister, she cleverly eliminated the ancient and evil tiger spirit, so that the witch could no longer prey upon innocent children in Taiwan.

THE BOY WHO DREW CATS

Japan

Another tale from the land of ailurophiles, Japan. The below version is based on the 1898 translation into English by Lafcadio Hearn, but the original story is said to date as far back as the fifteenth century.

A very long time ago, in a small village in rural Japan, there lived a farmer and his wife. The pair of them were very good people, but also very poor, and they had a number of children. With many mouths to feed, the couple struggled to feed them all. At the age of 14, the eldest son was strong enough to help his father, and the little girls soon learned to help their mother from a very young age, but the youngest child, a little boy, did not seem to be fit for hard work.

This young boy was very clever – more so than all his brothers and sisters – but he was small and not physically strong. People said he would never grow very big and so his parents thought it would be better for their youngest son to become a priest and not a farmer. One day, they brought him to the temple in the village and asked the old priest who lived there if he would make their little boy his acolyte and teach him all that a priest would need to know.

The old man spoke kindly to the boy but also asked him several tough questions. So clever were the answers that the priest agreed to take the young lad with him into the temple, turn him into his acolyte and educate him in the ways of the priesthood. The boy was a quick learner and swiftly picked up everything that the old priest taught him and, for the most part, he was very obedient. He did, however, have one fault. He was exceptionally fond of drawing cats during study-hours, even where cats ought not to have been drawn at all. Whenever he found himself alone, he would draw cats – in the margins of the priest's books, on all the screens of the temple, on the walls and on the pillars. No matter how often the priest told him that this was not right, the young boy did not stop drawing cats – he could not really help it. This boy had 'the genius of an artist', but wasn't quite fit to be an acolyte either – a good acolyte ought to study the scriptures.

One day, after drawing some very clever pictures of cats on a paper screen, the old priest took him aside. 'My boy,' he told him severely, 'you must leave this temple at once. You will never make a good priest, but perhaps you might become a great artist one day. Let me give you one last piece of advice, and make sure you never forget it. Avoid large places at night, instead keep to small ones.'

The poor boy didn't really understand what the priest meant by 'Avoid large places at night, instead keep to small ones'. No matter how he pondered, while he was gathering together his little bundle of clothes to get ready to leave, he could not understand those words, and he was afraid to speak to the priest again except to bid him farewell.

He left the temple full of sorrow and began to ask himself what he should do. If he returned home, he was certain his father would punish him for disobeying the priest, so he didn't dare to head home. Then suddenly, he remembered that in the next village, some 12 miles away, there was a very big temple. The boy had heard that several priests could be found there, and he made up his mind to venture forth and find them. Hopefully, he could be made their acolyte instead.

As it happened, the big temple in the next village was closed up, but the boy did not know this. The reason behind the closing of the temple was that a goblin had scared away all the priests and taken possession of the place. Although many brave warriors had entered the temple at night to try and kill the goblin, they had never been seen alive again.

The boy didn't know any of this, so he walked all the way to the village in the hope of being treated kindly and taken on as an acolyte by the priests. When he reached the village darkness had already fallen, and all the villagers were asleep. The boy could see the big temple atop a hill at the other end of the main street and, what's more, he saw there were lights emanating from the temple windows. It was rumoured that the goblin lit lamps every evening to attract lonely travellers to the temple to ask for shelter.

Seeing the light, the boy immediately went to the temple and knocked on the door. Inside the temple all was silent. He knocked again and again, but still nobody came to answer the door. At long last, he gave the door a gentle push and was pleased to find that it had not been properly fastened. The boy went inside and there he saw a lamp casting a soothing glow, but there were no priests to be seen.

The young boy figured a priest would be sure to turn up very soon, so he sat down and he waited. Looking around, he noticed to his surprise that everything in the temple was covered with a thick layer of dust and cobwebs. This made him feel certain the priests would be keen to have an acolyte such as himself to help keep the place clean. He thought it strange that they had allowed everything to get so dusty and rundown.

What pleased him most, however, were some big white screens, perfect for painting cats upon. Even though he was very tired, he couldn't resist looking for, and finding, a writing-box, and soon he'd ground some ink, and started to draw cats. He drew a great many cats upon the screens and then he started to feel very, very sleepy.

Just as he was about to lie down and sleep next to one of the screens, he suddenly remembered the priest's words: 'Avoid large places at night, instead keep to small ones.' The temple was very large and the boy was all alone. As he pondered these words, even though he wasn't quite able to understand them, he began for the first time to feel a little fearful and he resolved to seek out a small place where he could sleep.

After looking around the temple, he found a small cabinet with a sliding door. He sneaked inside and slid the door shut. Then he lay down and promptly fell fast asleep. At a very late hour he was woken up by the most dreadful noise – a noise of fighting and screaming. It was so terrible that he didn't even dare to look through the little crack of the sliding door, he just lay very still, holding his breath in sheer fright. The temple light went out, but the awful sounds continued, increasing in strength and the whole temple shook.

Finally, after what seemed like hours, silence prevailed, but the boy was too scared to move. Not until the light of the morning sun shone into the cabinet through the cracks of the little door did he move. Then he slowly and cautiously left his hiding place and looked around. The first thing he saw was that the floor of the temple was covered with blood. And then he saw, lying dead in the middle of the floor, an enormous, monstrous rat – a goblin-rat – the size of a cow or even bigger.

Who or what could have killed the goblin-rat? There was no man or other creature to be seen. Then the astonished boy spotted that the mouths of all the cats he had drawn the night before were red and dripping with blood. He realised that the goblin had been killed by the cats that he had drawn. And for the first time, he understood the words of the wise old priest, 'Avoid large places at night, instead keep to small ones'.

This young boy grew up to become a very famous artist. Some of the many cats he drew are still shown to travellers in Japan to this day.

THE PHANTOM BIG CATS OF AUSTRALIA

Although domestic cats arrived in Australia comparatively late, there are a number of folk tales and urban myths focusing on sightings of big cats. Some go as far back as the 1830s, while others are much more modern tales. Below is a selection of the best known of these big cats, from the Tantanoola Tiger to the Blue Mountains Panther. Sightings have been widely reported for decades, but evidence of the existence of these often shy, elusive and none-too-friendly big cats remains inconclusive.

Gippsland Phantom Cat

Tales of a big cat stalking the area of Gippsland in south-eastern Australia (in the state of Victoria on the borders of New South Wales) date back to the 1970s. Known as the Gippsland Phantom Cat or Gippsland Big Cat, there have been hundreds of sightings, right up to modern day, but the jury is out as to its origins. Usually shy and steering clear of humans, numerous more or less blurry photographs of the Gippsland Big Cat have nonetheless appeared over the decades. When, in June 2005, a local deer hunter shot a large, black cat near the town of Sale, this seemed to finally provide proof that big cats lived in the area. However, after DNA tests were carried out, it was concluded that the 'big cat' was in all likelihood a feral descendent of the domestic moggie. While experts agree that the famed Gippsland Big Cat is just a larger-than-usual cat, urban legend has it that it's descended from pumas brought over as mascots by the US Army during the Second World War and then released into the wild at the end of the war.

Tantanoola Tiger

Sightings of the so-called Tantanoola Tiger go much further back than the Gippsland Phantom Cat, with mentions of the 'tiger' as early as the 1830s. The best-known case, however, is from the 1890s, when the beast terrorising the community of Tantanoola was actually caught and killed. Arguably, it doesn't really deserve a mention in a feline folk tales book, as the ferocious beast turned out to be a wolf, not a big cat. However, the name 'Tantanoola Tiger' stuck, long after the wolf was captured, shot and, subsequently, rather poorly taxidermied. Stories of sightings get scarcer after the 1890s, but some have still been reported as late as the 1940s and 50s.

Blue Mountains Panther

The Blue Mountains Panther, aka the Lithgow Panther, is arguably the big cat that's received the most media attention throughout Australia. Sightings go back over 100 years and since the 1990s these have increased in frequency. In 2003, a teenage boy was attacked right by his own home by a large feline, which clawed his arms and stomach, leading to the boy getting so-called cat scratch fever from his injuries. Following this attack, the government carried out extensive research, but their conclusions remained vague. Although the existence and origins of the Lithgow Panther are still inconclusive, sightings continue, and the mystery of the cat's origins remains unsolved.

Grampian Panther or Puma

The so-called Grampian Panther or Puma is another well-known big cat mystery. It's been spotted in and around the Grampian National Park in the state of Victoria, where there have been sightings of one or more big cats for decades, essentially from the 1970s onwards. The national park covers a vast area and, consequently, it would be perfectly possible for big cats to live there undetected. Hikers and climbers have reported seeing big, puma-like cats on many occasions and in the 1970s and 80s studies were carried out to prove whether big cats were making the national park their home. Although both studies were inconclusive, big, puma-like cats are thought to be living in the Grampians and many of the sightings have been by forestry workers or industry staff who know the area well. Again, the cats' origins remain unknown.

WHY DOG AND CAT ARE ENEMIES

China

Another version of why cats and dogs came to be such sworn enemies (there is also an American version, 'Why Dogs Chase Cats' in the Americas section, page 48, and a more similar version from the Philippines, 'Why Dogs Wag Their Tails', earlier in this section, page 61). This version is from China and has a slight Lord of the Rings *quality about it, even though the trick here is to retrieve the ring, rather than dispose of it.*

Once upon a time, there lived a man and his wife and the couple had a ring of gold. This ring was a lucky ring and anyone who owned it was guaranteed to have enough to live on. The married couple, however, did not know this, and so they parted with the ring for a very small sum of money.

No sooner was the ring gone than the husband and wife began to grow poorer and poorer, until one day, they did not know when or how they would get their next meal. The couple had a dog and a cat, and these two were now forced to go hungry as well. Thus, the two animals began to discuss among themselves what they might do to restore their owners to their former good fortune.

At long last the dog came up with an idea. 'We must get the ring back again,' he told the cat.

'The ring has been carefully locked away in a chest, where no one can reach it,' the cat answered, not sounding hopeful.

'Then you must catch a mouse,' the dog continued, 'and persuade said mouse that it will need to gnaw a hole through the chest, sneak in and fetch the ring. And if she refuses to do so, tell her that you will bite her and scratch her to death if she doesn't comply and you will soon see that she will do what she's asked to do.'

The dog's idea pleased the cat, and she set about catching a mouse. She was swift and, mouse caught, the cat immediately headed for the house where the chest was kept with the mouse in her paw and the dog followed.

They reached a wide, flowing river. Since the cat could not swim, the dog allowed her, still with the mouse in her paw, to stay on his back as he swam across the waters. Safely across, the cat carried the mouse to the house where the chest was kept. The mouse, fearing for her life, did as she was told and gnawed a hole in the chest, sneaking in and successfully fetching the ring.

On their way back from the house with the chest, the cat put the ring in her mouth and returned to the river, where the dog was waiting for her. He then started swimming across the waters once more with the cat on his back. Together, they carried on towards home to return the lucky ring to their master and mistress.

The dog could only run along the ground, so when there was a house in their way he had no choice but to go around it. The cat, however, was far more agile and quickly climbed over the rooftops, thus reaching their home long before the dog did. Consequently, it was the cat who brought the ring to her master.

'What a good creature the cat is,' said the master to his wife. 'We will always give her enough to eat and care for her as though she were our very own beloved child.'

When the dog came home, the couple beat and scolded him, thinking he had not helped the cat to bring the ring back home again. All the while, the cat sat by the fireplace, contentedly purring and never betraying how matters truly stood. The dog grew frightfully angry at the cat who had robbed him of his rightful reward, and every time he saw her after that, he flew into a frenzy and chased her. Ever since that day, cats and dogs are enemies.

THE VAMPIRE CAT OF NABÉSHIMA

Japan

Monster cats, shapeshifting cats and werecats all crop up in Japanese folklore and folk tales. In this tale, a vampire cat shapeshifts into a beautiful woman with dangerous consequences for the prince in the story.

There is a traditional tale in the Nabéshima family that, many years ago, the Prince of Hizen was bewitched and cursed by a cat that had been kept by one of his retainers. This prince had in his house a lady of rare beauty, called O Toyo. Among all his ladies, she was the favourite, and none could rival her charms and accomplishments.

One day, the Prince went out into the garden with O Toyo and remained enjoying the fragrance of the flowers until sunset, when they returned to the palace, never noticing that they were being followed by a large cat. Having parted with her lord, O Toyo retired to her own room and went to bed. At midnight, she awoke with a start and became aware of a huge cat that crouched watching her. When she cried out, the beast sprang on her and, fixing its cruel teeth in her delicate throat, throttled her to death. What a piteous end for so fair a lady, the darling of her prince's heart, to die suddenly, bitten to death by a cat!

Then the cat, having scratched out a grave under the veranda, buried the corpse of O Toyo and, assuming her form, began to bewitch the Prince.

But my lord the Prince knew nothing of all this and would scarcely have believed that the beautiful creature who caressed and soothed him was a foul fiend that had slain his mistress and assumed her shape in order to drain his life blood. Day by day, as time went on, the Prince's strength dwindled away; the colour of his face changed and became pale and sickly – here was as a man suffering from a deadly sickness.

Seeing this, his councillors and his wife became so greatly alarmed that they summoned the physicians, who prescribed various remedies for him, but the more medicine he took, the more serious his illness appeared, and no treatment was of the slightest use. Most of all, he suffered at nighttime, when his sleep would be troubled and disturbed by hideous dreams.

In consequence, his councillors nightly appointed 100 of his retainers to sit up and watch over him, but towards ten o'clock on the very first night the watch was set, the guards were seized by a sudden and unaccountable drowsiness, which they could not resist, until one by one, every man had nodded off. Then the false O Toyo came in and harassed the Prince until morning.

The following night, the same thing occurred, and the Prince was subjected to the beast's tyranny, while his guards slept helplessly around him. Night after night this was repeated, until at last three of the Prince's councillors determined that they themselves would stay up and keep guard to see whether they could overcome this mysterious drowsiness, but they fared no better than the others and by ten o'clock they were fast asleep.

The next day the three councillors held a solemn conclave and their chief, one Isahaya Buzen, said, 'This is a remarkable thing, that a guard of 100 men should thus be overcome by sleep. For sure, the spell that is upon my lord and upon his guards must be the work of witchcraft. Now, as all our efforts have been to no avail, let us seek out Ruiten, the chief priest of the temple called Miyô In, and beseech him to hold prayers for the recovery of my lord.'

The other councillors approved of what Isahaya Buzen had said and they went to the priest Ruiten and engaged him to recite litanies so that the Prince might be restored to health. And so it came to pass that Ruiten, the chief priest of Miyô In, offered up nightly prayers for the Prince.

One night, at the ninth hour (midnight), when he had finished his religious exercises and was preparing to lie down to sleep, he fancied that he heard a noise outside in the garden, as if someone were washing himself at the well. Deeming this a strange occurrence, he looked down from the window. There, in the moonlight, he saw a handsome young soldier, some 24 years of age, washing himself. When he had finished cleaning himself and had put on his clothes, he stood before the figure of Buddha and prayed fervently for the recovery of his lord, the Prince.

Ruiten looked on with admiration. The young man, upon reaching the end of his prayer, was turning away to leave, but the priest stopped him.

'Sir, I pray you to tarry a little, I have something to say to you,' the priest called out.

'At your reverence's service. What may you please to want?' the young man answered.

'Pray be so good as to step up here and have a little talk,' said the priest.

'By your reverence's leave,' the young man answered, and with this, he went upstairs.

'Sir, I cannot conceal my admiration that you, being so young a man, should have so loyal a spirit,' the priest continued. 'I am Ruiten, the chief priest of this temple, engaged in praying for the recovery of my lord. Pray what is your name?'

'My name, sir, is Itô Sôda, and I am serving in the infantry of Nabéshima. Since my lord has been sick, my one desire has been to assist in nursing him, but, being only a simple soldier, I am not of sufficient rank to come into his presence, so I have no resource but to pray to the gods of the country and to Buddha that my lord may regain his health.'

When Ruiten heard this, he shed tears in admiration of the fidelity of Itô Sôda. 'Your purpose is, indeed, a good one,' he said, 'but what a strange sickness this is that my lord is afflicted with. Every night he suffers from horrible dreams and the retainers who sit up with him are all seized with a mysterious sleepiness, so that not one can keep awake. It is very extraordinary.'

'Yes,' replied Sôda, after a moment's reflection, 'this certainly must be witchcraft. If I could but obtain leave to sit up one night with the Prince, I would fain see whether I could not resist this drowsiness and detect the goblin.'

At last, the priest spoke again. 'I am in relations of friendship with Isahaya Buzen, the chief councillor of the Prince. I will speak to him of you and of your loyalty and will intercede with him that you may attain your wish.'

'Indeed, sir, I am most grateful. I am not prompted by any vain thought of self-advancement, should I succeed. All I wish for is the recovery of my lord. I commend myself to your kind favour.'

'Well then, tomorrow night I will take you with me to the councillor's house.'

'Thank you, sir, and farewell.'

And so they parted.

On the following evening, Itô Sôda returned to the temple Miyô In and, having found Ruiten, accompanied him to the house of Isahaya Buzen. Then the priest, leaving Sôda outside, went in to converse with the councillor and inquire after the Prince's health.

'And pray, sir, how is my lord? Is he in any better condition since I have been offering up prayers for him?' Ruiten asked.

'Indeed, no, his illness is very severe. We are certain that he must be the victim of some foul sorcery,' the councillor responded, 'but as there are no means of keeping a guard awake after ten o'clock, we cannot catch sight of the goblin, so we are in the greatest trouble.'

'I feel deeply for you – it must be most distressing,' Ruiten continued. 'However, I have something to tell you. I think that I have found a man who will detect the goblin and I have brought him with me.'

'Indeed! Who is the man?' The councillor was intrigued.

'Well, he is one of my lord's foot-soldiers,' said Ruiten. 'His name is Itô Sôda, a faithful fellow, and I trust that you will grant his request to be permitted to sit up with my lord.'

'Certainly, it is wonderful to find so much loyalty and zeal in a common soldier,' replied Isahaya Buzen, after a moment's reflection. 'Still it is impossible to allow a man of such low rank to perform the office of watching over my lord.'

'It is true that he is but a common soldier,' said the priest, 'but why not raise his rank in consideration of his fidelity and then let him mount guard?'

'It would be time enough to promote him after my lord's recovery,' the councillor countered. 'But come, let me see this Itô Sôda, that I may know what manner of man he is. If he pleases me, I will consult with the other councillors and perhaps we may grant his request.'

'I will bring him in forthwith,' replied Ruiten, who thereupon went out to fetch the young man.

When he returned, the priest presented Itô Sôda to the councillor, who looked at him attentively and was pleased with his comely and gentle appearance. 'So, I hear that you are anxious to be permitted to mount guard in my lord's room at night,' said the councillor. 'Well, I must consult with the other councillors, and we will see what can be done for you.'

When the young soldier heard this, he was greatly elated and took his leave after warmly thanking Ruiten, who had helped him to gain his objective.

The next day, the councillors held a meeting and sent for Itô Sôda, telling him that he might keep watch with the other retainers that very night. So, he went on his way in high spirits and at nightfall, having made all his preparations, took his place among the 100 gentlemen who were on duty in the Prince's bedroom.

Now the Prince slept in the centre of the room and the 100 guards around him sat keeping themselves awake with entertaining conversation and pleasant banter. But, as ten o'clock approached, one by one they all began to doze off where they sat and despite all their endeavours to keep one another awake, soon they were all fast asleep.

Itô Sôda, all this while, felt an irresistible desire to sleep wash over him, and though he tried by all sorts of ways to rouse himself, he saw that he would have no other recourse than resorting to an extreme measure, for which he had already made preparations. Drawing out a piece of oil paper, which he had brought with him, and spreading it over the mats, he sat down upon it. Then he took the small knife which he carried in the sheath of his dirk and stuck it into his own thigh. For a while the pain of the wound kept him awake, but as the slumber by which he was assailed was the work of sorcery, little by little he became drowsy again.

Then he twisted the knife round and round in his thigh, so that the pain was becoming very violent, thus proofing him against the feeling of sleepiness, and carefully kept a faithful watch. The oil paper which he had spread underneath his legs was to prevent the blood, which might spurt from his wound, from defiling the mats.

So Itô Sôda remained awake, but the rest of the guard slept, and as he watched, suddenly the sliding-doors of the Prince's room were drawn open and he saw a figure coming in stealthily, and as it drew nearer, he realised that the form was that of a marvellously beautiful young woman. Cautiously, she looked around her and when she saw that all the guard were asleep, she smiled an ominous smile and was going up to the Prince's bedside when she perceived that in one corner of the room there was a man still awake. This seemed to startle her, but she went right up to Sôda. 'I am not used to seeing you here. Who are you?' she said.

'My name is Itô Sôda and this is the first night that I have been on guard.'

'A troublesome office, truly! Why, here are all the rest of the guard asleep. How is it that you alone are awake? You are a trusty watchman.'

'There is nothing to boast about.'

'What is that wound on your knee? It is all red with blood.'

'Oh – I felt very sleepy, so I stuck my knife into my thigh and the pain of it has kept me awake.'

'What wondrous loyalty,' said the lady.

'Is it not the duty of a retainer to lay down his life for his master? Is such a scratch as this worth thinking about?'

Then the lady went up to the sleeping Prince and said, 'How fares it with my lord tonight?' but the Prince, worn out with sickness, made no reply.

But Itô Sôda was watching her eagerly and guessed that it was O Toyo and made up his mind that if she attempted to harass the Prince he would kill her on the spot. The goblin, however, which, in the form of O Toyo, had been tormenting the Prince every night and had come again that night for no other purpose, was defeated by the watchfulness of Itô Sôda. Whenever she drew near to the sick man, thinking to put her spells upon him, she would turn and look behind her and there she saw Itô Sôda glaring at her, so she had no choice but to go away again and leave the Prince undisturbed.

At last day broke, and the other officers, when they awoke and opened their eyes, saw that Itô Sôda had kept awake by stabbing himself in the thigh. They were greatly ashamed and went home crestfallen. That morning, Itô Sôda went to the house of Isahaya Buzen and told him all that had occurred the previous night.

The councillors were all loud in their praises of Itô Sôda's behaviour and ordered him to keep watch again that night. At the same hour, the false O Toyo came and looked all around the room and all the guard were asleep, except Itô Sôda, who was wide awake. And so, being again frustrated, she returned to her own apartments.

Now since Sôda had been on guard the Prince had passed quiet nights, so his sickness began to get better and there was great joy in the palace. Sôda was promoted and rewarded with an estate. Meanwhile, O Toyo, seeing that her nightly visits bore no fruit, kept away and from that time forth, the nightguard were no longer subject to fits of drowsiness.

This coincidence struck Itô Sôda as very strange, so he went to Isahaya Buzen and told him that of a certainty this O Toyo was no other than a goblin. Isahaya Buzen reflected for a while. 'Well, then, how shall we kill the foul thing?' he asked

'I will go to the creature's room, as if nothing were the matter and try to kill her, but in case she should try to escape, I will beg you to order eight men to stop outside and lie in wait for her.'

Having agreed upon this plan, Itô Sôda went at nightfall to O Toyo's apartment, pretending to have been sent with a message from the Prince. She saw him arrive and asked him, 'What message have you brought me from my lord?'

'Oh, nothing in particular. Be so kind as to look at this letter,' he said. As he spoke, he drew near to her and suddenly drawing his dirk cut at her, but the goblin, springing back, seized a halberd and glared fiercely at Itô Sôda.

'How dare you behave like this to one of your lord's ladies? I will have you dismissed,' she said and tried to strike Itô Sôda with the halberd. But he fought desperately with his dirk and the goblin, seeing that she was no match for him, threw away the halberd and from a beautiful woman, she suddenly transformed into a cat, which, leaping up the sides of the room, jumped onto the roof.

Isahaya Buzen and his eight men who were watching outside shot at the cat but missed it and the beast made good its escape. So, the cat fled to the mountains and did much mischief among the people in the surroundings, until at last the Prince of Hizen ordered a great hunt and the beast was killed.

The Prince recovered from his sickness and Itô Sôda was richly rewarded.

THE TWO CATS

Middle East

In this moral, cautionary tale warning of the dangers of avarice, a poor starved kitty does not fare well when lured off by a fellow feline to enjoy the feast at the Sultan's banquet. I can't help feeling rather sorry for this hapless, unlucky, scrawny little pussycat.

In former days, there was an old woman, who lived in a hut more confined than the minds of the ignorant and darker than the tombs of misers. Her companion was a cat, from the mirror of whose imagination the appearance of bread had never been reflected, nor had she from friends or strangers ever heard its name. It was enough that this cat, every now and then, scented a mouse or observed the print of its feet on the floor. When, blessed by favouring stars or benignant fortune, one fell into her claws, she became like a beggar who discovers a treasure of gold, her cheeks glowed with rapture and past grief was consumed by present joy.

This feast would last for a week or more and while enjoying it she was wont to exclaim to herself, 'Am I, oh God, when I contemplate this, in a dream or awake? Am I to experience such prosperity after such adversity?'

But as the dwelling of the old woman was, in general, the mansion of famine to this cat, she was always complaining and forming extravagant and fanciful schemes. One day, when reduced to extreme weakness, she reached the top of the hut after much exertion. From her lofty vantage point, she observed a cat stalking on the wall of a neighbour's house. Like a fierce tiger, this cat advanced with measured steps but was so loaded with flesh that she could hardly raise her feet. The old woman's companion was amazed to see one of her own species so fat and sleek, she could barely contain her astonishment.

'Your stately strides have brought you here at last; pray tell me from whence you come? From whence have you arrived with so lovely an appearance? You look as if you hail from the banquet of the *Khan of Khatai*. Where have you acquired such a comeliness? And how came you by that glorious strength?' she asked as she sat there atop the old woman's hut.

'I am the Sultan's crumb-eater,' the unknown cat replied. 'Each morning, when they spread the convivial table, I attend at the palace, and there exhibit my address and courage. From among the rich meats and wheat-cakes I cull a few choice morsels, then I retire and pass my time till next day in delightful indolence.'

The old lady's cat now wanted to know what rich meat was and what taste wheat-cakes had? 'As for me,' she added, in a melancholy tone, 'during my lifetime I have neither eaten nor seen anything but the old woman's gruel and the flesh of mice.'

'This accounts for the difficulty I have in distinguishing you from a spider,' said the other cat, smiling now. 'Your shape and stature are such as must make the whole generation of cats blush and we must ever feel ashamed while you carry so miserable an appearance abroad. You certainly have the ears and tail of a cat, but in other respects you are a complete spider. Were you to see the Sultan's palace and to smell his delicious viands, most undoubtedly those withered bones would be restored. You would receive new life, you would come out from behind the curtain of invisibility into the plane of observation.'

The old woman's cat addressed the other in the most supplicating manner. 'Oh, my sister,' she exclaimed, 'have I not the sacred claims of a neighbour upon you? Are we not linked in the ties of kinship? What prevents your giving a proof of friendship by taking me with you when next you visit the palace? Perhaps from your favour plenty may flow to me and from your patronage I may attain dignity and honour. Withdraw not from the friendship of the honourable, abandon not the support of the elect.'

The heart of the Sultan's crumb-eater was melted by this pathetic address. She promised that her new friend should accompany her on the next visit to the palace. The latter, overjoyed, went down immediately from the terrace and communicated every particular to the old woman, who addressed her with the following counsel, 'Be not deceived, my dearest friend, by the worldly language you have listened to and abandon not your corner of content, for the cup of the covetous is only to be filled by the dust of the grave and the eye of cupidity and hope can only be closed by the needle of mortality and the thread of fate. It is content that makes men rich. Mark this, ye avaricious, who traverse the world: he neither knows nor pays adoration to his God, who is dissatisfied with his condition and fortune.'

But the expected feast had taken such possession of poor puss's imagination, that the healing counsel of the old woman was discarded and ignored.

'The good advice of all the world is like wind in a cage, or water in a sieve, when bestowed upon the headstrong.'

The very next day, accompanied by her companion, the half-starved cat hobbled to the Sultan's palace. Before this unfortunate wretch arrived, as it is decreed that the covetous shall be disappointed, an extraordinary event had occurred, and owing to her evil destiny, the water of disappointment was poured on the flame of her immature ambition. As it happened, a whole legion of cats had, the day before, surrounded the feast and made so much noise that they disturbed the guests. In consequence, the Sultan had ordered that some archers armed with bows from Tartary should on this day be concealed, and whatever cat advanced into the field of valour, covered with the shield of audacity, should, on eating the first morsel, be overtaken by their arrows.

The old lady's poor pussycat was not aware of this order. The moment the flavour of the viands reached her, she flew like an eagle to the place of her prey. Scarcely had the weight of a mouthful been placed in the scale to balance her hunger, when a heart-dividing arrow pierced her breast. A stream of blood rushed from the wound.

She fled, in dread of death, exclaiming, 'Should I escape from this terrific archer, I will be satisfied with my mouse and the miserable hut of my old mistress! My soul rejects the honey if accompanied by the sting. Content with the most frugal fare is preferable.'

OLD MOUNTAIN UNCLE, THE TIGER WITHOUT MANNERS

Korea

This is a tale from the Kangwŏn/ Gangwon Province, which straddles the border between modern-day North and South Korea. Just as Taiwan has a 'Tiger Aunt', the Korean peninsula has its own 'tiger tale' – the tale of the 'Old Mountain Uncle'.

Tigers are seen in a very different light in this day and age – and their plight is well known – but many a tale hails from a time when hunting and killing tigers was common practice. This tale of trickery and deception echoes several other tales from different parts of the world, some of which are included in this collection.

'Mountain Uncle' was the name given by the villagers to a splendid striped tiger. This tiger lived among the highlands of Kangwŏn/ Gangwon Province, where the cliffs overlook the Sea of Japan. Hunters rarely saw him, and among his fellow tigers, the Mountain Uncle boasted that no matter how often he'd been shot at, he had never been wounded. And as for traps, this tiger knew them all and just laughed at the devices used by man to catch him to strip him of his much-coveted skin.

In summer he kept to the high hills and lived on the fat deer grazing there. In winter, when heavy snow, biting winds and terrible cold kept human beings indoors, old Mountain Uncle would head down to the villages. There he would prowl around stables, cattle enclosures or pigsties in the hope of catching and killing a young donkey, a fat calf or even a suckling pig. More often than not he succeeded, thus turning into the terror of the country for miles around.

As it happened, Mountain Uncle was rambling among the lower hills on a day in autumn. Even though he was far from any village, he continually kept a sharp lookout for traps and hunters, but could not spot any. He was very hungry and hoped to catch some game.

Upon rounding a huge rock, Mountain Uncle suddenly saw in his path ahead a great pair of paws – a big tiger, just like himself, he thought. Mountain Uncle stopped and twitched his tail in a most ferocious fashion as a challenge to the other tiger, growled menacingly and got ready to spring. Great was his surprise when he saw the other tiger doing exactly the same things. Mountain Uncle felt sure there would be a terrible struggle, but he didn't mind as, of course, he expected to win.

Mountain Uncle sprang forth and after a tremendous leap in the air, landed in a pit and in a heap, all bruised and disappointed. There was no other tiger in sight. Instead, a heavy lid of logs slammed shut over his head with a bang and there he lay in darkness.

Old Mountain Uncle was caught at long last. The hunters had concealed the pit with sticks and leaves. Then, covering the upright timbers with vines and brushwood, they had had hung a bit of looking glass on them. Although Mountain Uncle had often seen his own reflection in a body of water when stooping to drink, this time, not seeing any water, he was deceived. Mountain Uncle had truly believed there was another real tiger right there, wanting to fight him.

A little while later, a Buddhist priest, who believed in being kind to all living creatures, came walking along the path. Hearing an animal moaning, he opened the trap and, lifting the lid, saw Old Mountain Uncle sitting there at the bottom of the pit licking his bruised paw. 'Oh, please, Mr Man, let me get out, for I am badly hurt,' said the tiger to the priest.

The kind and caring priest lifted one of the logs and slid it down until it reached the bottom of the pit so that the tiger could climb up and out.

Old Mountain Uncle expressed his thanks thus, 'I am deeply grateful to you, sir, for helping me out of my trouble. Nevertheless, as I am very hungry, I must eat you up.'

The priest was very much surprised and indignant at such a vile display of ingratitude. He found this to be very bad manners and entirely against the law of the mountains, so he appealed to a big tree to decide between them.

The tree spirit spoke through the rustling leaves and declared that the man should go free and that the tiger was both ungrateful and had no manners. Old Mountain Uncle was hardly satisfied by this, especially as the priest was unusually fat and would make a very good dinner. However, he allowed the man one more appeal and this time to a big rock.

'The man is certainly right, Venerable Mountain Uncle, and you are wholly wrong,' said the spirit in the rock. 'Your master, the Mountain Spirit, who rides on the green bull and the piebald horse to punish his enemies, will certainly chastise you if you devour this priest. You will no longer be seen fit as a messenger of the Mountain Lord if you are so ungrateful as to eat the man who saved you from starvation or death in the trap. It is shockingly bad manners even to think of such a thing.'

The tiger felt deeply ashamed, but he was still feeling the ravishes of hunger. To be sure of saving his own skin, the priest proposed to make the toad a judge. The tiger agreed. The toad, with his gold-rimmed eyes, looked very wise indeed and instead of answering quickly, as the tree and rock did, he deliberated for a long time. The priest felt his heart sinking, while the tiger kept moving his jaws as if anticipating a great feast. He felt sure that Old Speckled Back would decide in his favour.

'I must go and see the trap before I can make up my mind,' said the toad, looking as solemn as a judge.

So, all three leaped, hopped or walked to the trap. The tiger, moving fast, was there first, which was just what the toad, who was a friend of the priest, wanted. Besides, Old Speckled Back was diligently looking for a crack in the rocks nearby. So, while the toad and the tiger were studying the matter, the priest ran off and saved himself within the monastery gates. When at last Old Speckled Back decided against Mountain Uncle and in favour of the man, he had no sooner finished his judgement than he hopped into the rock crevice and, crawling far inside, defied the tiger, calling him an uncouth brute and an ungrateful beast. 'I dare you to do your worst!' he cried out from his hiding place.

Old Mountain Uncle became so mad with rage and hunger that his usual cunning and stealth turned into stupidity. He clawed at the rock to pull it open to get at the toad to tear him to pieces. Old Speckled Back, safe within, just laughed at his efforts.

Unable to do any harm, the tiger flew into an even greater passion of rage. The hotter his temper grew, the more he lost his wit. Poking his nose inside the crack, he rubbed it so hard on the rough rock that he soon bled to death.

When the hunter came along, he marvelled at what he saw, but he was glad to get rich by selling the tiger's fur, bones and claws, for, in Korea, nothing sells so well as a tiger. As for the toad, he told several generations of his descendants the story of how he outwitted the Old Mountain Uncle.

THE CAT AND THE MICE

Tibet

A 'devious cat' tale, where the cat is not to be trusted after all. This is a Tibetan version of the old cat-and-mouse dynamic (see also the Palestinian story of 'The Cat as Holy Man', earlier in this section, page 67), where the mice fare rather well for a change.

Once upon a time, there was a cat who lived in a large farmhouse with a very great number of mice. For many years, the cat found no difficulty in catching as many mice as she wanted to eat, living a very peaceful and pleasant life. But the years went by, and the cat found that she was growing old and infirm. It was by now becoming increasingly difficult for her to catch the same number of mice as before. After carefully considering the best thing to do, one day she gathered all the mice together and, promising not to touch them, she addressed them thus. 'Oh, mice,' she said, 'I have called you together to tell you something. The truth is that I have led a very wicked life, and now, in my old age, I repent, and I am truly sorry for having caused you all so much inconvenience and annoyance. In the future, I aim to turn over a new leaf. From now on, it is my firm intention to devote myself entirely to religious contemplation and no longer molest you. Henceforth, you are at liberty to run about as freely as you will without needing to fear me. All I ask of you is that twice every day you should all file past me in procession and each one make an obeisance as you pass me by, as a token of your gratitude to me for my kindness.'

When the mice heard this, they were greatly pleased. They thought that now, at last, they would be free from all danger from their former enemy, the cat. So, unsuspecting, they very thankfully promised to fulfil the cat's conditions and agreed that they would file past her and show their gratitude twice a day.

When evening came, the cat took her seat on a cushion at one end of the room and the mice all went by in single file, each one making a gesture of gratitude as it passed. Now, the cunning old cat had thought up this little plan very carefully with an objective of her own. As soon as the procession had all passed by except for one little mouse, she suddenly seized the last mouse in her claws without anybody noticing what was happening and devoured it at her leisure. And so, twice every day, she seized the last mouse of the series and for a long time lived very comfortably without any trouble catching her mice at all and without any of the mice realising what was happening.

As it happened, among these mice there were two stalwart friends, whose names were Rambé and Ambé, who were very much attached to one another. These two were much cleverer and more cunning than most of the others. After a few days, they couldn't help but notice that the number of mice in the house seemed to be decreasing very much, in spite of the fact that the cat had promised not to kill any more.

So, they put their heads together and came up with a little plan for future processions. They agreed that Rambé was always to walk at the very front of the procession of the mice and that Ambé was to bring up the rear. All the time the procession was passing, Rambé was to call to Ambé, and Ambé was to answer Rambé at frequent intervals.

So, the very next evening, when the procession started as usual, Rambé marched along in front, and Ambé took up his position as the last mouse of them all. As soon as Rambé had passed the cushion where the cat was seated and had made his gesture of gratitude, he called out in a shrill voice, 'Where are you, Brother Ambé?'

'Here I am, Brother Rambé,' squeaked the other, from the rear of the procession.

And so they went on, calling out and answering one another until they had all filed past the cat, who had not dared to touch Ambé as long as his brother kept calling to him.

The cat was naturally very much annoyed by this, as she now had to go hungry that evening. Indeed, she felt very cross all night. But she thought it was only an accident which had brought the two friends, one in front and one at the rear of the procession. She hoped to make up for her enforced abstinence by finding a particularly fat mouse at the end of the procession next morning.

Imagine, then, her amazement and disgust when she found that on the following morning the very same arrangement had been made. Rambé called to Ambé and Ambé answered Rambé until all the mice had passed her and so, for the second time, she was robbed of her meal.

However, she disguised her feelings of anger as best she could and decided to give the mice one more trial. In the evening, she took her seat as usual on the cushion and waited for the mice to appear.

Meanwhile, Rambé and Ambé had warned the other mice to be on the lookout and to be ready to take flight the moment the cat showed any appearance of anger. At the appointed time, the procession started as usual and as soon as Rambé had passed the cat, he squeaked out, 'Where are you, Brother Ambé?'

'Here I am, Brother Rambé,' came the shrill voice from the rear.

This was more than the cat could stand. She made a fierce leap right into the middle of the mice, who were thoroughly prepared for her – and in an instant, they scuttled off in every direction to their holes. Before the cat had time to catch a single one, the room was empty and there wasn't a mouse in sight anywhere.

After this, the mice were very careful not to put any further trust in the treacherous cat, who died of starvation soon afterwards, unable as she was to procure any of her customary food. But Rambé and Ambé lived for many years and were held in high honour and esteem by all the other mice in the community.

THE BALDHEADED CAT OF KOWASHI

Japan

A rather scary 'bakeneko' *tale of a* yōkai, *who is a shapeshifting cat taking the form of an elderly lady.* 'Bakeneko' *literally means 'changed cat' and these shapeshifting, demon cats appear in many Japanese folk tales. Why this tale is called 'The Baldheaded Cat' remains a mystery, as there's no mention of the cat in the story being bald.*

Kowashi Kamon was a low-ranking samurai in the service of the Kyōgoku family in the province of Sanuki. Kowashi had an aging mother, 80 years of age, and they lived a simple, but happy life together in a respectable household. With the passing of time, however, Kowashi started to notice several unusual changes to his mother's behaviour.

Although she'd always had an aversion to fish, she now relished it, even crunching the fish bones. This made her son very puzzled, and his amazement grew greater still when one night he saw his mother dancing a curious dance on the veranda, seemingly with some invisible companions, her head covered with a handkerchief.

On a moonlit night a few months later, a fishmonger was climbing the mountain pass in the area on his way home after selling fish when he was suddenly attacked by a whole army of cats, coveting the fish that remained unsold in his basket. He fended them off with the pole he used to carry the basket. Seeing they were no match for the fishmonger, one of the cats said, 'Go and fetch the old woman of Kowashi'.

As the man knew who the old woman was, he thought this was very strange indeed. He swiftly climbed up a nearby pine tree and waited there, fearing and preparing for the worst. Before long, the army of cats, who were watching him from below, exclaimed, 'Oh, there she comes! The old woman of Kowashi.'

Along came an old and big cat with grey fur. She climbed up the very same tree where the fishmonger was sitting, approaching him slowly, inch by inch, her eyes glowing like red lanterns, her claws as sharp as knives. By a stroke of luck, the fishmonger had a hook to hand and, awaiting his chance, he whacked the great, grey cat's brow as hard as he could.

As the sky lightened in the east, the cats dispersed in all directions and the fishmonger was finally able to jump down from his perch up the pine tree. Hurrying back down the mountain pass, he went straight to Kowashi's house to tell him all that had happened.

'Ah, now I fully understand everything,' Kowashi Kamon whispered to his visitor. 'This morning, I noticed a mark on my mother's forehead. She told me that she had tripped in the garden and hit her head on a stone last night, but somehow, I doubt that very much.'

Kowashi examined his mother's wound and found it to match the fishmonger's description, so he killed the old woman with one fierce blow from his sword. There, at his feet, lay a big, old, grey cat in a pool of blood. The remains of his real mother, reduced to a skeleton, were discovered underneath the floorboards.

THE TIGER AND THE SHADOW

Malaysia

Tigers feature in these two tales from Malaysia. The first is similar to the Indian tale, 'The Lion and the Hare' (see page 58), and many others from across Asia and elsewhere, featuring a smaller animal tricking a big cat. In these tales, from Ulu Kedah near the border with Thailand, the trickster is a mouse-deer, or chevrotain, a species now feared extinct.

There was a saltlick in the jungle to which all the beasts of the forest resorted, but they were greatly afraid to venture there because of an old tiger who would kill one of them every single day. At length, therefore, P'lando', the mouse-deer, approached the tiger. 'Why not permit me to bring you a beast every day,' he said to the tiger, 'to save you from hunting for your food?'

The tiger consented, and P'lando' went off to make arrangements with the other beasts of the jungle. No matter how he tried though, he could not persuade any of them to be turned into the tiger's next meal and after three days he was forced to set off with nobody but Kuwis, the smallest of the flying squirrels.

'I could not bring you any of the other beasts because the way was blocked by a fat old tiger with a flying squirrel sitting astride its muzzle,' P'lando' said to the tiger upon arriving.

On hearing this, the tiger was mightily surprised. 'Let us go and find it and drive it away!' he exclaimed.

The three therefore set out, the flying squirrel now perched upon the tiger's muzzle and the mouse-deer sitting astride its hind quarters. On reaching the river, the mouse-deer pointed to the tiger's likeness in the water. 'Look there! That is the fat old tiger that I saw,' he cried out.

On hearing this, the tiger leapt into the river to attack his own shadow and was drowned immediately.

THE KING OF THE TIGERS IS SICK

Malaysia

The mouse-deer, rather than the tiger, takes centre stage in this cruel tale of cunning and trickery, featuring the king of all tigers and his unfortunate crown prince. Collected from the Tembeling River area.

When the great king of all the tigers was sick, the tiger crown prince made obeisance. 'If my lord will taste of the flesh of every beast of the field, peradventure my lord may recover,' he proclaimed.

The crown prince then commanded that every kind of beast be summoned into the king's presence and as they appeared, one by one, the king ate them. It was only the mouse-deer who, when summoned, refused to appear. This did not sit well with the great king, and his wrath was kindled against the mouse-deer. In the end, the mouse-deer too was fain to appear.

When he appeared, the king questioned him thus. 'Why did you not attend immediately when we had summoned hither every kind of beast that lives in the field?'

'Your humble servant could not approach Your Majesty because of a dream of certain medicine that would make your majesty well again,' the mouse-deer answered.

'What medicine was this of which you dreamed?' the king asked, intrigued.

'Your humble servant dreamed that the only remedy for Your Majesty's sickness was for Your Majesty to seize and devour that which is nearest your majesty.'

Immediately upon hearing this, the great king of the tigers seized the prince of the tigers and devoured him also. Straightaway, the king was cured, and the mouse-deer himself became crown prince in turn.

THE CAT WHICH COULD NOT BE KILLED

India

Another dog-versus-cat tale; this one from India. Although the tale doesn't tell us when, why or how the dog and cat became such enemies, the dog is so keen to kill his foe, the cat, that he tries all sorts of tricks and enlists the help of many different creatures, to no avail as it turns out – this resilient kitty remains quite impervious to harm. Or is she perchance a wildcat or even a tiger?

Once upon a time, there was a dog and a cat and the pair of them were always quarrelling. Even though the dog frequently beat the cat, he never did manage to hurt her. She remained unscathed and as cheerful as ever, prancing and dancing about.

'You could never hurt me. Oh no, you'd never hurt me one bit!' she would cry out. 'I *had* a pain in my shoulder, but luckily that's all gone away now.'

Thoroughly fed up, the dog went to a *mainá*. 'What shall I do to hurt this cat?' he asked. 'I beat her and I bite her, but nothing I do can hurt her. As you can see, I am a big dog and she is rather big too. Yet if I beat her she doesn't get hurt, but if she beats me she hurts me so much.'

'This is what you must do,' said the *mainá*. 'You must bite her mouth very, very hard, and this way you'll hurt her.'

'Oh, no,' said the cat, who had just turned up, laughing, 'that won't hurt me at all.'

The dog took the *mainá*'s advice and bit the cat's mouth as hard as he could.

'You could never hurt me. Oh no, you didn't hurt me one bit!' said the cat, prancing and dancing about as before.

Downcast and disappointed, the dog returned to the *mainá*. 'What shall I do?' he enquired again.

'This time, bite her ears,' said the *mainá*.

Said and done, the dog bit the cat's ears, but she just pranced and danced about.

'You could never hurt me. Oh no, you didn't hurt me one bit!' she said, 'And guess what? Now I can put earrings in my ears.' And the kittycat put earrings in her ears.

Even more disappointed and frustrated, the dog now went to the elephant. 'Can you kill this cat?' he asked. 'You see, she worries me and torments me so every single day.'

'Oh yes, of course I can kill her,' said the elephant. 'She is only little and I am enormous.'

The elephant charged at the cat, picked her up with his trunk, and threw her a long, long way. But the cat remained unhurt. Up she jumped at once, prancing and dancing about. 'You could never hurt me. Oh no, you never hurt me one bit! I *had* a pain, but now I feel quite well again.'

Then the elephant got cross.

'I'll teach you to dance a different dance,' he said, and he grabbed the cat, placed her on the ground and put his great big foot on her.

But the remarkable cat was not hurt at all. Instead, she was soon prancing and dancing about. 'You could never hurt me. Oh no, you didn't hurt me one bit,' she said and with that, she dug her claws deep into the elephant's trunk.

The elephant ran away screaming and when he got back to the dog he told him, 'You had better beware of that cat. She belongs to the tiger tribe.'

The dog was undeterred and very angry with the cat. 'What shall I do to kill this cat?' he asked himself. He bit her nose so hard that it bled, but she laughed at him.

'Well, now I can put a ring in my nose as well,' she said.

This drove the dog mad with rage. 'I will bite her tail in half,' he decided and so he bit her tail in half, and still he could not hurt her.

The enraged dog then went to the leopard. 'I will give you anything you want,' he said, 'if you can only kill my foe, the cat, who keeps prancing and dancing and laughing at me, making my life miserable.'

'Very well, I will kill her for you,' the leopard answered and together they went to the cat to finally kill her.

'Stop! Wait!' the cat said to the leopard, 'Let me talk to you, but first let me give you something to eat and then I will tell you what I have to say.'

With that, the cat ran off ever so fast and far. After she had run a mile she stopped running and started prancing and dancing about, while calling out to the leopard waiting for his food, 'I'll give you nothing to eat. Oh no! And you could never kill me!'

'What a clever cat that is,' the leopard told the dog, and went away ever so cross.

The dog, however, refused to give up and next he went to a man. 'Can you kill this cat; she troubles me so?' he asked the man.

'Why, of course I can,' the man said. 'I will stick this knife into her gut and I will kill her for you.' And the man stuck his knife into the cat's stomach, but the cat jumped up, her stomach closed, and she remained unscathed. Not even the man could kill her and so he went on home.

Finally, the dog went to see the bear. 'Can *you* kill this cat?' he asked. 'For I have tried everything and I can't kill her.'

'I will kill her,' the bear said. He stuck all his claws into the cat, but even this did not hurt her. Instead, the cat stuck her claws into the bear's nose so deep that he died on the spot.

The poor dog then became so very unhappy that he went and threw himself into a hole and there he died.

Meanwhile, the cat went off to spend time with good friends. They are undoubtedly still prancing and dancing about and laughing at the dog.

THE CATS' ELOPEMENT

Japan

Japan has more feline folk tales than any other nation included in this collection. Not all tales, nor all cats, are cute and cuddly, but the two cats portrayed in this tale are both of the sweetest disposition. There's a hint of star-crossed lovers about this tale, but unlike Romeo and Juliet, it has a much happier ending. The tale doesn't reveal what happened to the cats' original owners, who had to learn the hard way that cats will live as, and how, they please. As cat lovers will know, from time to time, cats up and leave, choosing a new home and new preferred humans.

There was once a very beautiful cat named Gon, who had fur as smooth and shiny as silk and the most magnificent green eyes. Gon belonged to a music teacher, who loved him dearly for his sweet temper and affectionate ways, and he would not have parted with his cat for the world.

Nearby, there lived another most beautiful little feline, with soft, fluffy fur, a pink button nose and large, soulful eyes. Her name was Koma and her mistress doted on her every bit as much as Gon's master doted on him.

One night, when both cats were out for an exploratory amble, they happened to meet and immediately fell deeply in love with each other. Gon and Koma could not bear to be parted, they both wanted to spend their whole lives together and they had a long, earnest miaow about it.

Gon returned to his master to beg him to please allow him to go and live with Koma. His master, sadly, was far too attached to Gon to even consider this new arrangement and couldn't bear the thought of parting with his beloved cat. In turn, Koma went to see her mistress to beg her to let her go and live with her dearest husband Gon, but it soon became apparent that this would be even less possible.

The cat owners were so afraid of losing their beloved cats that they kept them confined almost like prisoners, making it so difficult for Gon and Koma to see each other that they at long last made the difficult decision to leave their loving master and mistress and go out into the wide world to be together.

As any cat owner knows, to keep a cat who means to escape locked up is as easy as keeping quicksilver between your forefinger and your thumb. And so it was that one dark night, both cats quietly slipped away, slinking off together into the night.

Day after day they wandered, always together, finding food as best they could. They left their hometown far behind, travelling many miles until they made it all the way to the Imperial City. Here the pair of them strolled through the crowded, busy streets until they reached a great big park. This was the garden of the Imperial Palace, but the cats did not know this. Instead, they thought the park was a very pleasant place and they felt right at home – this would be a good place to live, they thought – and they sat down underneath a flowering tree and were tenderly grooming each other when they heard a terrible noise.

Barking and growling, a huge mastiff was coming right at them, ready to attack. Koma positively flew up the tree, while Gon turned to face the attacker and defend them both. Not that he would have had much of a chance against such a great big dog, so Koma raised her voice from the top of the tree and cried for help. Luckily, a palace servant heard her cries and came to chase the dog away with the help of a stick. Then he spotted Gon, sitting by the tree. He'd never seen such a pretty cat and he swiftly scoped him up and brought him to the Princess, who had her own palace in the Imperial Palace grounds.

The Princess was delighted with Gon and his lovely ways and couldn't bear to be parted from him. But where was Koma?

Whenever Gon was able to sneak away from his Princess, he searched for her everywhere and asked if anyone had seen his beloved, but no matter how he tried, he got no news of Koma. All he could do was hope and wait.

The Princess, too, had her troubles. She was being persecuted by a vicious serpent, who had fallen madly in love with her, and he was a truly dangerous and sinister suitor. Although her maids had been instructed not to let him in, he was cunning, and the maids were sometimes a tad careless.

One day, the Princess was sitting on her own, playing her *koto*, when she felt something sliding up her sash. It was the snake, who had sneaked in and was gliding up her body to plant a kiss on her cheek. The Princess screamed in fright and leapt backwards. Gon had been asleep on a cushion right beside her, but the screams woke him up. Quick as a flash, he was up and had seized the serpent by the neck. A harsh nip and a rough shake and there the serpent lay dead beside the Princess and would never bother her again. The Princess was so happy, she picked Gon up, kissing him and petting him and praising him to the skies.

After the killing of the nasty serpent, nothing was ever too good for Gon – the best food, the softest cushions in the best spots, kisses and cuddles all day long, and anything he could wish for. If he could only have found his Koma, he felt his life would be complete.

One day, as he was lying by the window looking out, he saw a huge tomcat bullying a little female feline. Enraged, Gon left his sunny spot on the windowsill and shot outside, where he saw off the big bully once and for all. Then he turned towards the little lady feline to make sure she was fine and could hardly believe his eyes when he saw that it was his very own Koma. The pair of them went into an absolute frenzy of joy, purring and rubbing and nuzzling. Gon then proudly led his wife to the palace, where they told the Princess the whole story of their adventures before he had come to live with her in the palace. The Princess was so moved she shed many tears and promised them that they would never ever be separated again.

Shortly afterwards, the Princess married a Prince, who came to live with her in her palace. The Princess told him the story of how Gon had saved her from the snake and of all the troubles and travails the cat couple had suffered to be able to be together. The Prince promised to value and cherish them as much as the Princess did.

Gon and Koma had many children and so did the Princess and Prince. They all played together happily as long as they lived.

KASHA – THE JAPANESE FIRE CAT

Japan

This chapter looks at the inspiration behind the fiery monster-cat that adorns the Feline Folk Tales' *cover and explores how a fire cart came to be depicted as a fire cat.*

Japan has a long history of 'cat superstitions' and cats are revered, but also feared, throughout the land. The so-called corpse-stealing *kasha* are found in Buddhist folklore and legends from across Japan. Some evidence suggests they may originally derive from Chinese folk tales featuring demon cats.

One of Japan's *yōkai* – supernatural beings or spirits – the *kasha* was originally depicted as a fire cart, or burning chariot, that carried the souls of the damned down to the underworld. By the sixteenth century, *kasha* had come to be seen as demon-like beings, whether taking animal or human form, and by the 1700s, legends of *nekomata* and *kasha* had started to merge, leading to the depiction of the latter as cats. *Kasha* are a type of *bakeneko*, or monster-cat, and they often appear accompanied by hellish flames and lightning. The flaming demon hellcat was first depicted by Toriyama Sekien (1712–88), who compiled the first *yōkai* encyclopaedia, *The Illustrated Night Parade of a Hundred Demons/ Illustrated Demon Horde's Night Parade* (1776). Sekien may simply have used his own imagination when he first created the cat illustration of the *kasha* for his book and there is much debate on the subject among scholars, but what is certain is that *kasha* depicted as cats becomes far more common after the publication of Sekien's work.

A *kasha* can be hard to spot because, according to folk belief, they are usually ordinary domestic or stray cats. It's believed that your everyday domestic moggies can evolve into *kasha* after living extraordinarily long lives or if they come into contact with the body or coffin of someone recently deceased. Their tails then grow increasingly long, and they begin to develop magical powers (cats' tails are occasionally cut short to avoid them turning into *kasha*).

Just like their mere mortal kitty cousins, *kasha* are, unsurprisingly, nocturnal by nature. They can live among humans without us ever suspecting there's a demon in our midst. At funerals, however, the *kasha* will reveal their true colours, transforming into fiery monster-cats, complete with glowing eyes, lethal claws and fearsome fangs. The *kasha* often target humans who were wicked, mean or miserly in life. They are said to appear at funerals, leap onto a coffin, tear it open and – growling, hissing and spitting – snatch the corpses of the dead right out of their coffins. Sometimes acting as wardens of hell in service of Raijin, the Thunder God, *kasha* carry the deceased off to the underworld in a fire cart, to be tortured as punishment for earthly sins.

In other tales, *kasha* are said to be more indiscriminate in their choice of corpses and drag away innocent victims, not just sinners.

The corpse might also be stolen for the *kasha's* own purposes, such as reanimating or eating it. Tales abound of those recently deceased who have been revived by the *kasha* and used as a sort of puppet on a string, manipulated by the monster-cat.

Once snatched, getting your loved one's remains back was said to be near enough impossible. Thus, to avoid this happening, a mock funeral would be staged before the real thing, to guard against prowling *kasha*. The coffin would be filled with rocks, sometimes a head-shaving razor would be placed on top of it or a bamboo cage built around it, to ensure that the *kasha* could not interfere with the dead body.

Kasha are known to be strong and fast, able to leap across the rooftops even when carrying a human corpse. They are said to be able to speak in a human tongue and grow very large. 'Don't let cats near dead bodies' is a common saying in Japan. If a cat gets close to someone who has recently passed away or even near their coffin, it is believed that person will rise again.

Stormy weather or thunder is thought to signify the arrival of these monstrous creatures. One story from the nineteenth century ('The Musings of Bōsō', 1833) recounts how a ferocious wind, followed by mighty rumblings of thunder and flashes of lightning, interrupted a funeral procession. It was the *kasha* swooping down to steal the corpse. In another story, potentially dating back to the Tensho era (1573–92), it's a fireball from the sky that interrupts the funeral (Snow Country Tales, 1837). In this tale, the *kasha* is defeated by a priest using his staff to beat back the monster-cat.

Many of the *kasha* tales have a religious element and feature priests, rooted as they are in Buddhist folklore. In modern-day Japan, different *yōkai* continue to form part of popular culture, appearing in films, anime and manga. Folk beliefs may have changed, but supernatural beings, such as the *kasha*, with strong roots in folklore endure even in today's Japan.

FELINE FOLK TALES OF EUROPE

With research that's come to light in recent years, the jury seems to be out in terms of where cats were originally domesticated – perhaps not in Egypt, as originally thought, but in the Middle East. What is certain, however, is that cats have an important place in European folklore and folk tales, going back centuries. Whether as heroes, villains or even demons, cats crop up more frequently in folk tales than most other animals. Although they haven't always fared well or been as well loved as in this day and age (this is particularly true during the Middle Ages), they have always merited attention.

Europe is the part of the world where my book research has yielded the most fruit by quite a stretch, perhaps in part because more tales have been documented and written down, making them easier to find. Possibly with the exception of Japan, it is Europe that has the widest variety of feline folk tales focused on the domestic cat. I have chosen to include nearly twenty, from different parts of Europe, in this compilation. Some are very well known, such as 'Dick Whittington and His Cat' and 'King o' the Cats' from England, 'Baba Yaga' from Russia, and the 'Bremen Town Musicians' from Germany. Others are more obscure, even if known locally or nationally in their places of origin. Below, you will find stories that are funny, sad, scary and romantic, tales of bravado and derring-do, evil cats, clever cats, naughty cats, shapeshifting cats – European feline folk tales provide a wonderful mix of all of the above and more.

DICK WHITTINGTON AND HIS CAT

England

This rags-to-riches tale is perhaps the most famous cat tale of all in the United Kingdom. Arguably based on a true story, it is at the very least true that there was a person named Richard Whittington (c. 1354–1423) who did become Mayor of London. The story only appeared in writing some 150 years after the key character's death and historical facts surrounding the story are sketchy. Did he actually own a cat? The jury is out …

Once upon a time in England (for this all happened in England), there lived a poor orphan boy called Dick Whittington. One day, he overheard some men talking outside the local tavern.

'I hear the streets of London are paved with gold,' said one of the men.

'Oh,' Dick thought to himself, 'if I were to go to London, I could take some of all that gold from the street and make my fortune.'

Dick gathered together his few belongings, put them in a bag and set off for London. When he got to London, he soon discovered that the streets weren't paved with gold at all. In fact, they were covered in yucky dirt. Things were not going to plan and sadly, the young boy didn't have any money to return home. He began asking around for some work, but nobody wanted to take on a poor boy from the country.

At last, Dick Whittington's first day in the capital came to an end and the stars began to twinkle in the sky. He looked around for a place to sleep, but the only place he could find was the doorstep of a large house. As soon as he had settled himself down to sleep, the cook of the house came running out.

'Oh, no, no, no, no, no! No raggamuffins here on my doorstep. Be off with you, I say. Be off!' And with that, she started hitting him with the broom.

She'd just about chased him off when the master of the house, Alderman Fitzwarren, arrived home. 'Cook? What on earth is going on?'

'Oh, sir,' the cook moaned, sounding guilty. 'I'm just getting rid of this raggamuffin off the doorstep. I'm sure he's up to no good.'

Alderman Fitzwarren looked at the boy, who was looking all ragged and dirty and skinny, and he suddenly felt saddened and gloomy to see a child similar in age to his own in such a sorry state. 'What is your name, boy?' he asked.

'Dick. Dick Whittington, sir,' the boy replied.

'And are you a good worker?'

'Oh, yes sir, I certainly am, sir.'

The Alderman pondered for a moment or two.

'Cook,' he said, turning to the cook, 'we need a new boy in the kitchen. Take young Dick here and give him a wash and new clothes. Then in the morning, show him what needs to be done in the kitchen.'

'Of course, sir," said the Cook with smiles and a curtsy, but as soon as the Alderman was gone, she hit Dick with the broom again.

After spending the day working hard in the kitchen (and trying to avoid being hit with the broom), Dick had to climb to the top of the house to sleep on the floor in the dusty old attic. Just as he was falling asleep, mice and rats came out to creep and crawl all over his bed. One even tried to set up home in his boot! Poor Dick barely slept a wink.

The following morning, he went to work feeling really, really, really tired. He got hit with the broom rather a lot that day, as he was too tired to duck.

At the end of that long week, all the staff got paid. Dick took his money and went straight to the marketplace. He looked at all the fantastic things for sale: fruit and vegetables, cloths and textiles, horses and farm animals, leather, bowls and utensils, clothes and even hats – everything could be found here. Eventually, he found the stall he was looking for – a pet stall.

'I need a cat!' Dick cried, slightly hysterical from a lack of sleep. 'A cat who can get rid of all the mice and rats that crawl over me every night. Do you have one?'

'I do,' the pet seller replied. She could tell just by looking at him that Dick wouldn't have much money and cats are expensive, but she had a kind heart, so she asked him what his budget was.

'I have one shiny gold coin,' Dick proclaimed.

'What a nice coincidence,' said the seller. 'That's exactly how much this lovely ginger cat costs, and he's a really good mouser.' She gave him the cat in exchange for the coin, not letting on that the cat actually cost a lot more.

Dick and the cat instantly became best friends. That night, when Dick went up to bed, he took his cat with him. The mice and rats didn't stand a chance against such a fabulous feline.

Dick slept like a log every night while the cat was busy chasing away all the rats and mice. With all that sleep he was getting, he was finally better able to duck and dodge the Cook's broom.

One day, Alderman Fitzwarren's daughter, Alice, came into the kitchen to look for an apple. He helped her find one and they soon got talking, as they were about the same age. Sometimes, Dick was allowed to go out into the backyard and play games with Alice for a while. Then she would go back inside and return to her pastimes whilst Dick had to work hard in the kitchen.

'One day, I'm going to make something of myself,' Dick would say, when he thought no one was listening. 'And when I'm old enough, I'm going to marry Alice.' Lost in these daydreams, he frequently wouldn't hear the approaching footsteps and so got whacked on the head with the broom again.

'That'll teach you to daydream,' the Cook laughed. 'Back to work, you lazy, good-for-nothing raggamuffin.'

One day, Alderman Fitzwarren called all his staff to his study. 'As most of you know, I make a trip overseas every year to sell goods to the kings in North Africa. They pay a pretty penny for things that we can get easily here in London, as they can't get them in their homeland. Do any of you have anything you wish me to sell?'

Each member of staff offered up their goods and wares. Finally, the Alderman turned to Dick. 'Do you not have anything to sell Dick? It could make your fortune.'

'Alas, no sir. I don't have anything in the world except my cat.'

'Well, you'd get a pretty penny for her, I can tell you. The kings of North Africa have a terrible problem with rats and mice. It could make you a terrific fortune.'

Dick thought about what the Alderman had said. If he sold his cat, he would have enough money to become a tradesman and maybe even marry Alice. But his cat was his best friend, and without her, he wouldn't be able to sleep at night.

While Dick was um-ing and ah-ing, the cat walked into the study and purred around the Aldermans legs. Dick took it as a sign. 'Very well,' he said. 'Take the cat and sell her. But please make sure she goes to a nice family.'

'That I will, of course,' said the Alderman, and he smiled a Dick with a fatherly grin. 'Cook, while I'm away, will you look after Dick?'

'Of course, I will,' smiled the Cook. But when the Alderman wasn't looking, she scowled at Dick and wafted her hand under her nose, as if to say he was smelly.

Life got harder for Dick. Without his cat, he barely slept a wink, and the Cook took full advantage with her broom. His poor body was covered in bumps and bruises, and he missed his feline friend terribly.

Months went by and the Alderman did not return. Dick tried to buy another cat, but the seller had moved to a different market and he didn't know how to find her. Life, in other words, was grim.

Dick decided that living in London was too hard, and he would return home to Gloucestershire. One morning, before the rest of the household woke up, he put his belongings in his knapsack and headed out of London. He got as far as Highgate Hill when the bells of London started to chime. They didn't seem to be ringing their usual tune. Dick stopped and listened, and he heard the bells saying:

Turn again, Whittington
Lord Mayor of London
Turn again, Whittington
Thrice Mayor of London.

'The bells can talk! Dick shouted, but nobody heard him, he was all alone. 'And they're telling me to return to London to become Lord Mayor. Three times! Could it be real? I don't know, but I think I want to. If the bells said it, then it must be magic. Surely?'

Dick finally stopped having this conversation with himself and headed back into London. He braced himself, fully expecting a scolding from the Cook, before stepping into the kitchen. But there was no one there. The staff and the family were at the front of the house, greeting the Alderman, who had finally returned from his journey.

As Dick stepped out to meet him, the Alderman cried out, 'Dick, come and join me! I sold that cat of yours.'

'To someone nice?' Dick asked.

'To someone very nice. A king, in fact. Your cat gets to eat the finest food and sleep on the plumpest cushions. The King paid a whole bag of gold for her. You're rich!'

'I'm rich?'

'You're rich!' the Alderman exclaimed.

'I'm rich!' Dick said.

'He's rich? the Cook asked.

'Yes!' the Alderman cried.

'Well, I always said he'd do well. He's always been one of my favourites,' the Cook lied, but no one was really listening to her anymore.

Dick got himself a trade, and when he was old enough, he did indeed marry Alice Fitzwarren. As the bells had told him that fateful day, he did become the Lord Mayor of London three times, and they all lived *Happily Ever After*, including the cat.

WHEN THE GOVERNOR'S CAT SET FIRE TO THE CITY OF UMEÅ

Sweden

The city of Umeå in the north-east of Sweden has a history of devastating fires. In 1888, the entire old town centre, including the governor's residence, burnt down. This tale, focusing on the key role played by a cat's tail, is an imaginative attempt at explaining what caused the great fire, while also poking fun at the local governor. Tales of cats and fires are also widespread in Japan.

The governor of the region of Västerbotten was travelling and had just reached the mountains near Sorsele. There he met an old woman with a remarkable animal sitting right by her side. 'What kind of creature is that?' said the governor.

''Tis a cat, 'aven't you ever seen a cat afore?' the old woman replied.

Well, the governor hadn't, as a matter of fact. He really liked that old woman's little feline and so it happened that he decided to buy the cat from her. She was given a horse and cart as payment. Mightily pleased with her bargain, the old woman left the cat and drove off.

That's when the governor realised he'd forgotten to ask her what cats eat, so he rushed after her. The old woman thought he'd changed his mind and simply drove on ever faster to get away. In the end, the governor had to cry out to her from a great distance. 'What does the cat eat?' the governor shouted.

'He'll eat what he gets given,' the old woman shouted in reply.

Unfortunately, the governor was a bit hard of hearing and instead he heard 'he'll eat the goats he's given'. Back in the city of Umeå, where the governor resided, the cat was solely given plenty of goats to eat.

This, however, made the cat very angry indeed and he kept scratching his new master, so that the governor had scrapes and cuts and wounds all over.

Unfortunately, scratching a governor is a capital offence, and most definitely not allowed, so the kitty needed to be punished. He was sentenced to death by burning. They set fire to birchbark and put the cat atop the flames.

The birchbark wound itself around the kittycat's tail, but the cat wasn't planning on staying put to get burnt to a crisp. No, he set off across the rooftops, burning birchbark still wound around his tail, jumping from rooftop to rooftop, thus setting fire to all the wooden houses of Umeå.

To end this cat tale, kitty is said to have escaped the fire intact, tail and all, and then settled somewhere with far better food than those goats that he was given at the governor's residence. He may well be living in his new home still, growing more rotund and content each day.

THE HERON, THE CAT AND THE BRAMBLE

Wales

A sweet little explanatory tale from Wales. Ever thought bramble was tricky to get past? Now you know why...

Once there was a heron and a cat and a bramble. The three were farming.

And they gave up farming and shared the money between them – between the three.

And what did the heron do but put the money in a purse round its neck and saw its reflection in the river as he flew above it. And the string broke and it lost the purse. And ever since then, the heron has been looking for the purse along the river.

And the cat bought wheat with its money, and the mice ate it all. And that's why the cat's ferociously hostile towards the mice ever since.

And the bramble lent its money to some stranger and didn't know who he was. And that's where it is – taking hold of every man who passes it, thinking that that's the man it gave its money to.

THE CAT AND THE MOUSE SET UP HOUSE

Germany

This Brothers Grimm tale of the devious cat and the poor, trusting mouse has many versions, including one entitled 'The Cats and the Christening' from the Shetland Islands, written in dialect, one published by Philip Pullman (Grimm Tales: for Young and Old) *and many others. This version is based on the 1884 translation by Margaret Hunt.*

A cat had made the acquaintance of a mouse and was so eloquent about the great love and friendship that he felt for her that the mouse at last agreed that they should live and keep house together. 'We must make preparations for winter, or else we shall suffer from hunger,' said the cat, 'and you, little mouse, cannot venture out everywhere, or in the end you will be caught in a trap.'

This good advice was followed, and they bought a pot of fat, but they did not know where to store it. 'I know of no place where it will be better stored than in the church,' the cat finally said after much deliberation. 'No one dares take anything from there. We will put it beneath the altar and not touch it until we are in need of it.'

So, the pot was stored safely away, but it wasn't long before the cat began to greatly long for it and said to the mouse, 'I wanted to tell you, little mouse, that my cousin has brought a baby boy into the world, and she has asked me to be his godfather. He is white with brown spots, and I am to hold him over the baptismal font. Let me go out today, and you look after the house by yourself.'

'Yes, of course,' answered the mouse, 'by all means, go, and if you get anything good to eat, think of me. I would like to drink a drop of sweet red christening wine myself.'

All this, however, was untrue. The cat had no cousin and had not been asked to be godfather. He went straight to the church, crept up to the pot of fat, began to lick at it and licked off the top of the fat. Then he went for a stroll on the roofs of the town, looked out for opportunities and then stretched out in the sun, licking his whiskers whenever he thought of the pot of fat. He did not return home until it was evening.

'Well, here you are again,' said the mouse. 'You must have had a happy day.'

'Everything went well,' answered the cat.

'What name did they give the child?' asked the mouse.

'Top-Off,' said the cat quite coolly.

'Top-Off?' cried the mouse. 'Why, that is a very odd and uncommon name. Is it a usual one in your family?'

'What does that matter?' said the cat. 'It is no worse than Crumb-Thief, as your godchildren are called.'

Before long the cat was seized by another serious fit of craving. 'You must do me another favour,' he said, turning to the mouse, 'and once more manage the house alone for a day. I have again been asked to be godfather, and since the child has a white ring around its neck, I cannot refuse.'

The good mouse consented. The cat, however, crept behind the town wall to the church and devoured half the pot of fat. 'Nothing tastes as good as that which one eats by oneself,' he said and was quite satisfied with his day's work.

When he arrived home the mouse asked, 'What name was this child christened with then?'

'Half-Gone,' answered the cat.

'Half-Gone? What are you talking about? I have never heard that name in all my life. I'll wager it is not in the almanac.'

It wasn't long before the cat's mouth began to water yet again for the delicious goods. 'All good things come in threes,' he said to the mouse. 'I have been asked to be godfather again. The child is totally black, only it has white paws. Otherwise, it has not a single white hair on its whole body. This only happens once every few years. You will let me go, won't you?'

'Top-Off, Half-Gone,' answered the mouse, 'they are such odd names, that they make me stop and think.'

'Here you sit at home,' said the cat, 'with your dark grey fur coat and long braid of hair fantasising. This is because you never go out in the daytime.'

During the cat's absence, the mouse cleaned the house and put it in order, while the greedy cat devoured all the rest of the fat. 'One only feels a sense of peace after everything has been eaten,' he said to himself.

Well filled and fat, he did not return home until nighttime. The mouse immediately asked what name had been given to the third child.

'You will not like this name either,' said the cat. 'His name is All-Gone.'

'All-Gone!' cried the mouse. 'That is the most worrisome name of all. I have never seen it in print. All-Gone! What can it mean?' Then she shook her head, curled up, and lay down to sleep.

From this time onwards, no one invited the cat to be godfather, but when winter came and there was no longer anything to eat to be found outside, the mouse thought of their stash of stored food. 'Come, cat,' she said. 'We will go to our pot of fat that we have kept for ourselves. It will taste good now.'

'Yes,' answered the cat. 'You will enjoy it as much as you would enjoy sticking that dainty tongue of yours out of the window.'

They set out on their way, but when they arrived, the pot of fat, to be sure, was still in its place, but it was empty.

'Alas,' said the mouse, 'now I see what has been happening. Now it comes to light. You are a true fiend. You ate everything when you were pretending to be godfather. First top off, then half gone, then …'

'Be quiet!' cried the cat. 'One more word, and I will eat you too.'

'All gone' was already on the poor mouse's lips. She had scarcely spoken it before the cat sprang at her, seized her and swallowed her up. You see, that is the way of the world.

THE LEGEND OF THE PUSSY WILLOW

Poland

There are many European and Native American folk tales and legends about the fluffy, grey catkins of the pussy willow tree. Here is a sweet little tale from Poland explaining how catkins came about.

An old Polish legend tells the story of how, many, many springtimes ago, a poor mother cat was desperately crying and miaowing at the bank of the river. Her tiny, helpless kittens had one by one fallen off the riverbank and into the river while chasing butterflies. Now they were all running the risk of getting swept away by the waters and drowning in the river.

The majestic willows lining the riverbank heard the mother cat's desolate meows and vowed to help her. The trees leaned out across the flowing river, sweeping their long, graceful branches down to the water's surface to rescue the tiny kittens where they had fallen in. Each kitten gripped the branches tightly with their tiny claws and the branches of the willows safely brought them back to shore.

Every springtime since, legend has it that the willow branches sprout tiny furlike buds where the kittens once clung.

KING O' THE CATS

England

There are many slightly different versions of this tale, including 'The Death of Kasserikus' from Sweden (see later in this section, page 146) and 'The Death of Knurre-Murre' from Denmark. In the Scandinavian versions, the cat is sometimes described as a shapeshifting troll. The English tale dates as far back as the fifteenth century, while one of the best-known versions – Beware the Cat *– was written by William Baldwin in 1553 and published a few years later.*

One cold, dark winter evening, the sexton's wife was sitting by the fireplace with her large black cat, Old Tom, right next to her. They were both dozing as they sat there awaiting the arrival of the husband, but he didn't come. They waited and they waited and then, at long last, he came rushing in, shouting, 'Who is Tommy Tildrum?', looking so wild and frantic that both wife and cat stared at him in surprise, wondering what on earth might be the matter with him.

'Why, what's wrong, dear?' his wife asked. 'Why do you want to know who Tommy Tildrum is?'

'Oh, you wouldn't believe what an adventure I've just had,' her husband answered. 'I was digging down at old Mr Fordyce's grave and I guess I must have fallen asleep. I only woke up when I heard this loud sound, like a cat's *miaou*.'

'*Miaou*!' said Old Tom, the cat, in answer.

'Yes, that's it. Just like that,' said the husband. 'So, I peeked up over the edge of the grave and what do you think I saw?'

'How should I know?' his wife answered.

'I saw nine black cats, just like our Old Tom here, all with a white spot on their chests. And guess what they were carrying – a small coffin with a black velvet pall and on the pall was a small coronet of gold. Every third step they took, they all cried as one: *miaou*.'

'*Miaou*!' said Old Tom again.

'Yes, just like that,' said the husband. 'And as they got closer and closer to me, I could see them quite distinctly because their eyes shone with a sort of green light. They all came towards me, there were eight of them carrying the coffin and the biggest cat of all was walking in front and … But look at our Old Tom and how oddly he's looking at me. It's as though he can understand exactly what I'm talking about.'

'Go on, go on,' said his wife impatiently. 'Never you mind Old Tom now, continue your tale.'

'Right, as I was saying, they were coming right towards me, slowly and solemnly, and every third step they cried together, *miaou* …'

'*Miaou*!' said Old Tom, yet again.

'Yes, just like that, till they came to a halt opposite Mr Fordyce's grave, right where I was digging. And then they stood quite still and looked straight at me. I did feel odd, I swear, I did. But look at Old Tom, he's looking at me just now in the same way that they did.'

'Go on, go on,' said his wife, even more impatiently than before. 'Never you mind Old Tom, continue with your tale.'

'Right, now where was I? Oh yes,' the sexton continued, 'they stood there looking at me and then the biggest one who wasn't carrying the coffin came forward and, staring straight at me, he spoke to me in a squeaky voice: "Tell Tom Tildrum that Tim Toldrum's dead," he said and that's why I asked you just earlier if you knew who Tom Tildrum was, for otherwise, how can I tell Tom Tildrum that Tim Toldrum is dead, if I don't know who Tom Tildrum is?'

'Look at Old Tom! Look at Old Tom!' his wife screamed suddenly.

They both looked in surprise at Old Tom, who was swelling and staring and at last cried out, 'What? Old Tim is dead? Then I am the King o' the Cats!' And with that, Old Tom rushed up the chimney and was never seen again.

THE KITTY ON DOVREFJELL MOUNTAIN

Norway

In this Christmas tale of trolls from Finnmark, the northernmost province of Norway, the cat isn't strictly speaking a cat, but luckily for Halvor, the troublesome trolls never find out.

Once upon a time, there was a man up in Finnmark who had caught a large, white bear, which he was going to take to the King of Denmark.

It so happened that he came to Dovrefjell Mountain on Christmas Eve. He went to a cottage where there lived a man whose name was Halvor, and he asked the man for lodging for himself and his white bear. 'God bless us,' said Halvor, 'but we can't give anyone lodging just now, for every Christmas Eve the house is so full of trolls that we are forced to move out ourselves and we'll have no shelter over our own heads, to say nothing of providing for anyone else.'

'Oh' said the man, 'if that's the only trouble, then you can very well let me use your house. My bear can sleep under the stove here and I can sleep in the storeroom.'

Well, he begged and pleaded so convincingly that at last he got permission to stay there overnight. The people of the house moved out, but before they left, everything was made ready for the trolls. The table was set with creamy porridge and fish and sausages and everything else that was good, just as for any other grand feast.

When everything was ready, in came the trolls. Some were large and some were small. Some had long tails and some had no tails at all. And some had long, long noses. They ate and drank and partook of everything.

Then one of the troll youngsters saw the white bear lying under the stove, so he took a piece of sausage, stuck it onto a fork and went and poked it against the white bear's nose, burning it. 'Kitty, do you want some sausage?' he shrieked.

The white bear rose up, fiercely growling and then chased the whole pack of trolls out, both large and small.

A year later, Halvor was out in the woods at midday of Christmas Eve, gathering wood for the holidays, for he expected the trolls again. As he was chopping, he heard a voice shouting from the woods, 'Halvor! Halvor!'

'Yes?' Halvor replied.

'Do you still have that big cat?'

'Yes,' Halvor said. 'She's lying at home under the stove and what's more, she now has seven kittens, far bigger and fiercer than she is herself.'

'Then, we'll never come to your place again,' the troll in the woods shouted back, and ever since that time the trolls have never eaten their Yule porridge with Halvor on Dovrefjell Mountain again.

THE CAT, THE COCK AND THE FOX

Ukraine

In this tale from Ukraine, the cat has to repeatedly rescue his stalwart companion, the cock. The foxes, usually known for their cunning, end up being tricked by the clever feline, while cock makes a miraculous recovery after his roasting.

There was, once upon a time, a cat and a cock who agreed to live together, so they built themselves a hut on an ash-heap, and the cock kept house while the cat went foraging for sausages.

One day the fox came running up.

'Open the door, little cock,' cried she.

'Pussy told me not to, little fox,' said the cock.

'Open the door, little cock,' repeated the fox.

'I tell you, pussy told me not to, little fox,' said the cock again.

At last, however, the cock grew tired of always saying 'No', so he opened the door and in rushed the fox, seizing him in her jaws and running off with him.

Then the cock cried out:

Help! Pussy-pussy!
That foxy hussy
Has got me tight
With all her might
Across her tail
My legs do trail
Along the bridge so stony!

The cat heard the cry for help, gave chase to the fox, rescued the cock, brought him home, and scolded him well. 'Now keep out of her jaws in the future,' said the cat, 'if you don't want to be killed altogether.'

Then the cat went out foraging for wheat, so that the cock might have something to eat. He had scarcely gone when the sly she-fox again came creeping up.

'Dear little cock,' said she, 'pray open the door.'

'Nay, little fox. Pussy said I wasn't to do so.'

But the fox went on pleading and persuading till at last the cock let him in. Then the fox rushed at him, seizing him by the neck, and running off with him.

The the cock cried out:

Help! Pussy-pussy!
That foxy hussy
Has got me tight
With all her might
Across her tail
My legs do trail
Along the bridge so stony!

The cat heard the cry for help and again he ran after the fox, rescued the cock and gave the fox a sound drubbing. 'Now, mind you never let her come in again,' said the cat to the cock, 'or she'll eat you.'

But the next time the cat went out, the she-fox came again.

'Dear little cock,' she said, 'open the door'

'No, little fox! Pussy said I wasn't to do so.'

But the fox begged and begged so piteously that, at last, the cock was quite touched and opened the door. Then the fox caught him by the throat again, and ran away with him, and the cock cried out:

Help! Pussy-pussy!
That foxy hussy
Has got me tight
With all her might
Across her tail
My legs do trail
Along the bridge so stony!

The cat heard the cry for help and gave chase again. He ran and he ran, but this time he couldn't catch the fox up.

He returned home and wept bitterly, because he was now all alone. At last, however, he dried his tears and got himself a little fiddle, a little fiddle-bow, and a big sack and went to the fox's hole and began to play:

Fiddle-de-dee!
The foxy so wee
Had daughters twice two,
And a little son too,
Called Phil. Fiddle-dee!
Come, foxy, and see
My sweet minstrelsy!

'Mummy, I'll go out and see who it is that is playing so nicely,' said the fox's daughter. Out she skipped, but no sooner did pussy see her than he caught hold of her and popped her into his sack. Then he played again:

Fiddle-de-dee!
The foxy so wee
Had daughters twice two,
And a little son too,
Called Phil. Fiddle-dee!
Come, foxy, and see
My sweet minstrelsy!

Then the second daughter skipped out, and pussy caught her by the forehead and popped her into his sack too.

He went on playing and singing till he had got all four daughters into his sack and the little son also. The old fox was left all alone and she waited and she waited, but not one of them came back. At last, she said to herself, 'I'll go out and call them home, for the cock is roasting, and the milk pottage is simmering, and 'tis high time we had something to eat.'

Out she popped and the cat pounced upon her and killed her too. Then he went and drank up all the soup and gobbled up all the pottage, and then he saw the cock lying on a plate.

'Come, shake yourself, cock,' said puss.

So, the cock shook himself and got up, and the cat took the cock home, and the dead foxes too. And when they got home, they skinned them to make nice beds to lie upon and lived happily together in peace and plenty.

And as they laughed over the joke as a good joke, we may laugh over it too.

THE CLEVER KITTY

Sweden

Cats in folk tales are often given magical powers of some kind. This is a tale of a shapeshifting cat who can talk and even outwit a giant, from the region of Bohuslän on the west coast of Sweden. The story is reminiscent of Hans Christian Andersen's 'The Princess and the Pea' and it's one of many stories from prolific local storyteller August Jakobsson (1844–1930). He collected tales and songs during his journeys buying and selling lobster along the coast and many of his stories were documented in 1919–20 by David Arill.

There was once a crofter who had two children, a son and a daughter. Then, suddenly the crofter and his wife died, leaving the boy and girl orphaned. The two children decided to split their inheritance, for they could not stay in the little old house and all that remained for them to share between them was a cow and a cat. The girl was very disgruntled when she realised all she'd be getting was the cat.

'Do not be disheartened,' said the kitty, 'for, truly, you have got the best end of the bargain.'

The two siblings set off into world, in different directions. The young lad went off with his cow, and the girl and the kitty went the opposite way. When they had walked a fair distance, the girl and the kitty reached the king's abode. This is where the prince spotted her, for this girl was strikingly beautiful. The prince asked her where she hailed from.

The kitty was quick to advise her. 'Say that you're from such and such a castle,' the cat swiftly whispered to the girl.

As fate would have it, the two young people – the girl and the prince – got married and the kitty-cat taught the girl well. She was well rehearsed and always able to tell them that whatever finery they showed her, what she had back home in her own castle was much finer still.

The queen thought her very posh indeed. When she made the bed for the princess, she added two or three bits of straw amongst the bedding. In the morning, the queen asked, 'So did you sleep well last night?'

'No, not at all,' the princess replied, 'I feel as though I've slept on large tree trunks.'

It was the kitty who had taught her to say that, you see. The princess confessed that she actually slept much, much better at home in her own castle.

The following evening, the queen made the girl's bed again and added three or four peas amongst the bedding. In the morning the queen asked her if she had slept well.

'No,' said the princess, 'I feel as though I've slept on large stones!'

'She must be terribly refined and elegant,' the queen thought to herself.

Soon the prince and princess were off to visit the grand castle. When they'd driven for a little while, the kitty set off ahead of the couple, spotting lots of fine-looking farm animals along the way. 'There are a few people following in my footsteps,' the cat said to the shepherds looking after the animals. 'When they ask who the owner of the fine animals is, tell them they belong to the new princess.'

When the prince saw the fine-looking creatures, of course he asked who they belonged to.

'They belong to the new princess,' said the shepherds.

The couple drove on. Kitty ran on in advance. They reached some beautiful farmland with crops growing high. People were there harvesting the crops. The kitty approached them and said, 'Look, there's the prince driving by. If he asks who owns this bountiful farmland, say, "It belongs to the new princess".'

When the prince arrived, he duly asked who this bountiful farmland belonged to and was told that it belonged to the new princess.

On they drove, with the kitty always running ahead. There was a great big, beautiful castle, where an enormous giant lived. When the kitty-cat arrived at the castle, the giant had gone out and locked the door.

'This would be a good time to turn into an ant,' said the kitty, and no sooner had she said it than she turned into an ant, crawled through the keyhole and inspected the castle.

The giant had gone out, but he could only do so after sunset, so this all happened at night. Time passed and dawn was approaching. The giant's heavy footsteps could be heard outside – he was returning.

'This would a good time to turn into a loaf of bread,' the kitty said, and swiftly turned into a loaf of bread inside the keyhole.

The giant came to unlock the door, but no matter how he tried, he couldn't get the key into the hole. The sun began to rise …

The kitty cried out, 'Beautiful maiden to the east!' and when the giant turned to look, the sun shone right at him and he burst.

The clever kitty managed to move the giant out of the way just in time for the arrival of the prince and the princess. Never before had the prince seen such a marvellous castle as this one.

WHY THE MANX CAT HAS NO TAIL

Isle of Man, United Kingdom

I was given this imaginative take on the story of how the Manx cat lost its tale by US-based storyteller David Thompson from Texas. In popular folklore, the tail was lost when the cat boarded Noah's Ark, but the heroic cat in this tale has a very different adventure on the Isle of Man, in the Irish Sea.

Have you ever wondered why a Manx cat has no tail? Well, here's a story that just might explain why.

Old Thomas was a cat who lived on the Isle of Man in the Irish Sea, the body of water between England, Wales and Ireland. Well, anyway, Thomas was the beloved cat of an old couple who had a small but comfortable home on the island. He was not just a house cat, he was also the guardian of the house, or so he convinced himself.

Thomas was a great mouser, keeping this home free from them and loving his quiet, yet busy home. The old man and old woman – who, by the way, belonged to him, or so he had convinced himself – loved Thomas very much and always stroked and petted and held him in their laps around the much-used woodburning stove that heated the home.

Now, the old man and woman were well known for their eggs and milk and butter and often went into town to sell their wares. When they left the house to go to market, they would always tell Thomas to guard the house and make certain that nothing untoward happened while they were away. Thomas would always meow his agreement and wait for their return, for they always brought him some sort of treat.

One day, the man and woman told Thomas that they were going to the market and that he was in charge, so to speak, while they were gone. Thomas meowed and rubbed himself up against their legs, followed them to the door and then jumped up on the windowsill to watch them leave. He then curled himself up on the sill, basking in the sunshine.

It was while the old man and old woman were away that two not-so-honest men snuck up to the door to see if anyone was home. Seeing that the house was empty, or so they thought, they pushed the door open and entered, thinking there had to be something inside that they could steal.

Well, as soon as the door was pushed open, Thomas woke up from his mid-morning nap and saw what was happening. And sure as shooting, he slowly, quietly, waited to pounce on the robbers. I mean, after all, he was the house guardian and took his job quite seriously, as only a cat can.

When the robbers entered the main room, Thomas pounced with claws extended and a loud screech. He landed directly on the face of one of the robbers, slashing with his claws, then jumped onto the other robber's face. I tell you, it was definitely a row and a half. Slashing with claws, biting whatever he could and screeching like a banshee, Old Thomas was.

The robbers were very much taken by surprise and pushing Thomas off their bodies as best they could, they headed for the door while Thomas gave chase. However, the door closed on Thomas's tail and snapped it clear off, all the way to his hind legs.

The old man and old woman came home later that day and saw that Thomas didn't have his tail anymore. They nursed it, gave him as many treats as he wanted afterwards, and praised him greatly for his bravery and courage. As a gift to Thomas, they had also brought home a lovely lady cat to keep him company. It turned out that the family of kittens were all born without tails, but that didn't matter to the old man and old woman, to Thomas, nor to Leticia, the female cat.

And so, when you see cats with no tails, you can rest assured that Thomas was the father and ancestor of all Manx cats.

THE BREMEN TOWN MUSICIANS

Germany

There are numerous documented versions of this Grimm Brothers folk tale of friendship and cunning from places as far apart as Norway, South Africa, Spain, Finland and the United States. The version included here is adapted from the original tale collected by the Grimm Brothers.

A man had a donkey, who for many long years had untiringly carried sacks to the mill, but whose strength was now failing, so that he was becoming less and less able to work. His master thought that he would no longer feed him, but the donkey thought that it was not a good omen, and he ran away, setting forth on the road to Bremen, where he thought he could become a town musician.

When he had gone a little way, he found a hunting dog, who was panting like one who had run himself tired, lying in the road. 'Why are you panting so, Grab-Hold?' asked the donkey.

'Oh,' said the dog, 'because I am old and getting weaker day by day and can no longer go hunting, my master wanted to kill me, so I ran off. Now how should I earn my bread?'

'Do you know what?' said the donkey. 'I am going to Bremen and am going to become a town musician there. Come along and take up music too. I'll play the lute and you can beat the drums.'

The dog was satisfied with that and off they went together. It didn't take long before they happened upon a cat, sitting by the side of the road and making a face like three days of rainy weather. 'What has crossed you, old Beard-Licker?' said the donkey.

'Oh,' answered the cat, 'who can be cheerful when he risks losing his neck? I am getting on in years and my teeth are less sharp, so I would rather sit behind the stove and purr than chase after mice.

Therefore, my mistress wanted to drown me, but I took off. Now good advice is scarce and hard to come by. Where should I go?'

'Come with us to Bremen. After all, you understand night music. You can become a town musician there,' said the donkey and the dog. The cat agreed and went along with the pair of them.

The three refugees came to a farmyard, and the rooster of the house was sitting on the gate crying with all his might.

'Your cries pierce one's marrow and bone,' said the donkey. 'What are you up to?'

'I just prophesied good weather,' said the rooster, 'because it is Our Dear Lady's Day, when she washes the Christ Child's shirts and wants to dry them; but because Sunday guests are coming tomorrow, the lady of the house has no mercy and told the cook that she wants to eat me tomorrow in the soup, so I am supposed to let them cut off my head this evening. Now I am going to cry at the top of my voice as long as I can.'

'Hey now, Red-Head,' said the donkey, 'instead come away with us. We're going to Bremen. You can always find something better than death. You have a good voice and when we make music together, it will be very pleasing.'

The rooster was happy with the proposal and all four of them went off together. However, they could not reach the city of Bremen in one day and in the evening they came into a forest, where they decided they would spend the night. The donkey and the dog lay down under a big tree, but the cat and the rooster took to the branches. The rooster flew right to the top, where it was safest for him. Before falling asleep he looked around once again in all four directions, and he thought that he saw a little spark burning far off in the distance. He crowed to his companions that there must be a house not too far away, for a light was shining.

'Then we must get up and go there,' said the donkey, 'because the lodging here is poor.'

The dog said that he could do well with a few bones with a little meat on them.

Thus, they set forth towards the place where the light was shining. They soon saw it glittering more brightly and it became larger and larger, until they reached the front of a brightly lit robbers' house.

The donkey, being the largest of them, approached the window and looked in.

'What do you see, Gray-Horse?' asked the rooster.

'What do I see?' answered the donkey. 'I see a table all set with good things to eat and drink, while the robbers are sitting there all around it, enjoying themselves.'

'That would be something for us,' said the rooster.

'Ee-ah, ee-ah, oh, if we were only there, inside,' said the donkey.

The animals discussed how they might drive the robbers away, and at last they came up with a plan. The donkey was to stand with his front hooves on the window, the dog to jump up onto the donkey's back, the cat to climb onto the dog, and finally the rooster would fly up and sit on the cat's head.

When they had done that, at a signal they began to make their music all together. The donkey brayed, the dog barked, the cat meowed and the rooster crowed. Then they crashed through the window into the room, shattering the panes.

The robbers leapt up at the terrible bellowing, thinking that a ghost was entering their house, and they all fled into the woods in terror. Then the four companions seated themselves at the table and freely partook of the leftovers, eating as if they wouldn't see food for many weeks.

When the four minstrels had finished eating and drinking, they put out the light and looked for a place to sleep, each according to his nature and desire. The donkey lay down on the manure pile, the dog behind the door, the cat on the hearth next to the warm ashes and the rooster sat on the beam of the roof. Because they were tired from their long journey, they soon fell asleep.

When midnight had passed and the robbers saw from a distance that the light was no longer burning in the house and everything appeared to be quiet, their leader said, 'We really shouldn't have let ourselves be chased off like that'. He told one of them to go back and investigate the house.

The one they sent found everything to be peaceful and quiet, so he went into the kitchen to strike a light. He mistook the cat's glowing, fiery eyes for live coals and held a sulphur match next to them, so that it would catch fire. But the cat didn't think this was funny and jumped into his face, hissing, biting and scratching. The robber was terribly frightened and ran towards the back door, but the dog, who was lying there, jumped up and bit him in the leg. When he ran across the yard past the manure pile, the donkey gave him a healthy kick with his hindleg and the rooster, who had been awakened from his slumber by the noise and was now alert, hollered from the beam, 'Cock-a-doodle-doo!'

The robber ran as fast as he could back to the leader.

'Oh, there is a horrible witch sitting in the house!' he cried. 'She blew at me and scratched my face with her long fingers. And there is a man with a knife standing in front of the door and he stabbed me in the leg. And a black monster is lying in the yard. It struck at me with a wooden club. And not only that, but the judge is sitting up there on the roof, and he was calling out, "Bring the rascal here!" at the top of his voice. Then I did what I could to get away.'

From that time onwards, the robbers never dared return to the house. However, the four Bremen Town Musicians liked it so well there that they never left it again.

And the person who just told that story? I'll wager his mouth is still warm.

THE HOUSE OF KATHOLM

Denmark

A cat tale from Denmark, cleverly explaining how a place – Katholm or Cat Islet, near Grenå, in Jutland – got its name. It echoes the well-known English tale, 'Dick Whittington and His Cat' (see page 112), the Italian tale of 'Two Kind Cats', and many tales of ships' cats. There is indeed a large stately home at Katholm to this day, built in the late sixteenth century, but I've found no evidence that it's related to this tale.

There was once a man from Jutland who had made a lot of money through dishonest means. When he died, he decided to leave his ill-gotten gains equally between his three sons. The youngest of the three got his share and thought to himself, 'What comes with sin goes with sorrow' and, in consequence, he decided to submit his money to the water test. It was his belief that the ill-gotten money would sink to the bottom, while that which had been honestly acquired would float to the top.

Said and done, he threw all his money into the water, and only one solitary farthing floated up to the surface – that's how dishonest his father's ways had been. With this sole coin he bought himself a cat.

The pair of them went to sea, visiting foreign lands. After travelling far and wide, they happened upon a place where the people were plagued by huge numbers of rats and mice. As his cat had by then had kittens, who all turned out to be good mousers, he acquired great wealth selling them to the local population. In fact, they gave him so much gold that when he returned to Jutland, he was able to build himself a lovely house and he called it Katholm – Cat Islet – as he had made his fortune, all thanks to the aid of cats.

KING CAT

Hungary

A greedy cat who likes his milk gets thrown out of house and home, but being a clever and cunning con-artist-kitty, he soon invents a whole new life for himself, tricking all manner of creatures in this Hungarian cautionary tale of what can happen if you let fear get the better of you.

Once upon a time, there was a poor widow who lived by herself with a large tomcat for company. Although elderly, this tomcat was still very playful and as fond of treats as any little kitten might be. One morning, he even lapped up all the milk that had been left in a pan and the old widow got so mad at him that she severely chastised him and then sent him packing.

The poor old tomcat hid at the edge of the village right by a bridge, feeling sorry for himself. What was he to do?

At the other end of the bridge there sat the fox, Reynard, his bushy tail swinging merrily. Spotting the cat, he was mightily startled and fair leapt up and spun right round. Tom, too, took fright, his fur bristling. It was some time before either moved, since Reynard had never seen a cat and Tom had never before set eyes on a fox. Both felt terribly apprehensive and neither knew what to do.

Reynard, the fox, finally plucked up the courage to address the cat and he spoke thus: 'No offense intended, but may I ask what clan you belong to?'

'I am King of Cats,' Tom announced, thinking on his feet.

'King of Cats? I've never heard of him!'

'Never heard of him? Well, you ought to have. Didn't you know that so great is my power that I can make any animal instantly obey me.'

Reynard's fear only increased upon hearing this statement and he humbly invited the old tomcat into his abode for a nice bite of chicken.

It was coming up to midday and Tom really could do with some food, so he didn't need to be asked twice, and they set off for Reynard's lair.

Tom easily slipped into his royal role and very much enjoyed the fox respectfully waiting on him, as though he were indeed a real royal, speaking little and eating lots. After enjoying lots of tasty chicken, in true cat fashion, he curled up and fell asleep, as was his habit, giving the fox strict instructions to make sure he wasn't disturbed during his nap time.

Reynard obediently stood guard at the entrance to the lair when a rabbit skipped and hopped by.

'Hey there, bunny,' Reynard barked at him. 'You'd better keep away from here. My Lord King Cat is asleep just now and if he comes out, you won't know what's hit you. So great are his powers that he can make any animal instantly obey him.'

The little rabbit hopped off as quick as anything, stopping off at a quiet spot to rack his brains and contemplate. 'King Cat?' he said to himself. 'Nope, never heard of him.'

Master Bruin, the bear, just happened to pass by while the rabbit was sitting there thinking.

'And where are you off to, Master Bruin?' the rabbit asked.

'Oh, nowhere in particular. I was just feeling a little bored and thought I'd take an amble, that's all.'

'You'd better not go any further, for Reynard, the fox, says his Lord, King Cat, is asleep over there and if he comes out you won't know what's hit you, because so great are his powers that he can make any animal instantly obey him.'

'King Cat? Never heard of him! Wonder who the devil he might be. I'm going to go and see for myself who this "King Cat" might be.' And with those words, Master Bruin set off for Reynard's lair.

'Hey there, Master Bruin,' the fox barked at the bear. 'You'd better keep away from here. My Lord, King Cat, is asleep just now and if he comes out, you won't know what's hit you. So great are his powers that he can make any animal instantly obey him.'

When thus spoken to, Master Bruin completely lost his courage and silently returned to Bunny, the rabbit, who was in the company of Uncle Wolf and Sir Crow. They too had been turned away and all of them were venting and fuming.

'Who might this King Cat be? We've never heard of him!' they were saying, all talking at once. They all wanted to get a good look at him and agreed that the best way to go about was to invite him to dinner. Sir Crow was sent to deliver the invitation.

Reynard, the fox, saw Sir Crow approaching again and got very angry indeed. 'Get out of here! Haven't I told you my Lord, King Cat, is asleep just now and if he comes out, you won't know what's hit you. So great are his powers that he can make any animal instantly obey him.'

'I know, I know,' Sir Crow countered, 'but I've been sent by Master Bruin, Uncle Wolf and Bunny to invite you both to dine with them tomorrow.'

'I see ... Well, that is different. Please wait here a moment,' said Reynard, much appeased.

Reynard went into the lair to talk to King Cat and soon reemerged to let Sir Crow know that King Cat was happy to accept the invitation and the two of them would be delighted and honoured to come for dinner, if Sir Crow could let them know where they must go.

'I shall come for you tomorrow,' said Sir Crow, 'and I will show you the way.'

When hearing the good news, Master Bruin, Uncle Wolf and Bunny started preparing a slap-up meal, with Bunny as head chef as he had the shortest tail and was the least likely to get burnt. As Master Bruin was the strongest, it fell to him to bring firewood and game, while Uncle Wolf laid the table and turned the spits roasting over the open fire.

All was set, dinner was ready, and Sir Crow flew off to fetch the guests.

Arriving near the lair, he called out to the fox from a nearby tree branch.

'Just a minute, just a minute!' came the flustered reply. 'We're nearly ready, His Majesty is just twirling his moustache.'

Not long after, King Cat made his appearance. He was doing his utmost to move with stately grace and decorum, but if truth be told, he was rather scared of Sir Crow.

The crow was equally frightened of King Cat and just kept glancing at him out of the corner of one eye, as he flew from branch to branch, showing the guests the way.

Meanwhile, Bunny, Bruin and Wolf were eagerly awaiting their arrival, full of excitement, wondering what King Cat might be like. Every two seconds they were looking in the direction Sir Crow had flown, full of impatience and apprehension.

'Oh, there they are. They are coming!' Bunny cried out, in fright. They were all so frightened that chaos ensued … Bunny ran straight into the fire, Master Bruin ran straight into a tree, splitting the trunk in two, and Uncle Wolf shot off with the roasting spit and Sir Crow followed their example.

And so, the hungry guests found neither hosts, nor fabulous feast, but luckily, by the time they arrived Bunny had been thoroughly roasted in the fire, so they could pull him out and get some supper.

And if they haven't died yet, King Cat and Reynard are living happily to this day.

THE DOG, THE CAT AND THE MOUSE

Romania

This folk tale from Romania explains how dogs, cats and mice came to be such sworn enemies, despite having clear job descriptions to start off with. The Devil crops up as well in this tale, playing devil's advocate, as it were. There are similar tales from many different parts of the world (see also 'Why Dogs Chase Cats', in the Americas section, page 48, and 'Why Dogs Wag Their Tails' and 'Why Dog and Cat are Enemies, in the Australasia section, pages 61 and 77).

In the beginning, there was no enmity between the cat and dog, they lived on friendly terms together and served their master (Adam) faithfully, each one doing their own work. But as you know, it is very much better to have a written agreement from the start than to have a row afterwards, so they decided to draw up an agreement defining the work that each had to do. They decided that the dog was to do the work outside the house and the cat the work inside. For greater safety, the dog agreed that the cat should take care of the agreement, and the cat put it in the loft.

After some time had gone by, the Devil, who could not allow peace to last for a long time, was determined to set the dog up against the cat and whispered in his ear … And so it was that one day the dog remarked to the cat that he was not being treated fairly. He did not see why he should have all the trouble outside the house. Why should he be the one to have to watch for thieves and protect the house, suffer from cold and rain, while only getting scraps and bones for food? Sometimes he even got nothing at all. Meanwhile, the cat had all the comfort, purring and enjoying herself, near the hearth in warmth and safety.

'Well, an agreement is an agreement, and this is the agreement we made,' said the cat.

'Then let me see that agreement,' countered the dog.

The cat went quickly up to the loft to fetch the agreement, but the agreement, which had been a little greasy, had been nibbled by the mice who were living in the loft. They had gone on nibbling away until nothing was left of it but a heap of paper fluff. As this fluff was as soft as down, the mice made their home in it. When the cat came up and saw what the mice had done, her fury knew no bounds. She pursued them madly, killing as many as she could seize and running after the others, hellbent on catching them.

When the cat came back downstairs, the dog asked her for the agreement and, as the cat had not brought it, the dog, taking hold of her, shook her until he got tired of shaking her.

Ever since that time, whenever a dog meets a cat, he asks her to see the agreement and as she cannot show it to him, he goes for her and attacks her. The cat, knowing what the mice did to her, chases them whenever she sees them and catches and kills them whenever she can.

THE DEATH OF KASSERIKUS

Sweden

Black cats have a long history of being associated with black magic and witchcraft. In this Swedish version of the British tale 'King o' the Cats' (see page 124), from the region of Västmanland in central Sweden, the black cat in the story might just turn out to be the king of troll mountain.

Over in Skinnskatteberg, there is a story of an old farmer and his wife, who lived at Ställberget Mountain. One day, the old man walked past another mountain nearby, Dromborgsberget. Suddenly, he thought he could hear voices crying out deep inside the mountain. The old man stopped in his tracks and stood there listening to the sound of these strange cries, trying to discern what they might be saying.

Back home, he was greeted by his wife, who was sitting by the hearth in the centre of the room with their large, black cat curled up beside her.

'Would you believe,' said the old man, 'I heard such strange cries coming from inside that mountain yonder? At first, it just sounded like an odd noise, but then I distinctly heard them calling out: "Ask Måns to return home, Kasserikus is dead".'

As soon as the farmer had uttered these words, Måns, their large, black, male cat, who'd been fast asleep next to the old woman, woke up with a start. Quick as a flash, he leapt out of the open window, and ran, full pelt, towards Dromborgsberget Mountain.

No one ever saw the kittycat Måns again from that day onwards. The old couple became convinced that Måns was, in fact, an enchanted cat, who had now been called back home to take over as king of troll mountain after the death of his rival, Kasserikus.

THE WHITE CAT OF ÉCIJA

Spain

A tale of Moors and Christians from Andalusia in southern Spain, complete with a curse, several knights in shining armour and a shapeshifting white cat. It's arguably more of a fairy tale than a folk tale, but the cat does take centre stage – and who doesn't like a happy ending?

From the gates of the palace, situated on a gentle eminence in the vicinity of Écija, down to the banks of the Genil, the ground was covered with olive trees and the wild aloes formed a natural and strong fence around the property of the White Cat of Écija, whose origin, dating back to the days of Saracenic rule, was unknown to the liberated Spaniard. There was a great mystery attached to the palace and its occupants. Although the servants of the White Cat were, to all appearances, human beings, as they were deaf and dumb and would not, or could not, understand signs, the neighbours had not been able to discover the secret behind the mystery.

The palace was a noble building, in the style of the *alcázar* at Toledo, but not quite as large. The garden at the rear was laid out with many small lakes, around which, short distances apart, there stood beautifully sculpted statues of young men and women, who seemed to be looking sorrowfully into the water. Only the head and hand of an exceptionally gifted artist could have approached perfection so as to make the statues look as if alive. At night strings of small lamps were hung around the lakes, and from the interior of the palace came flowing strains of sweet, but very sad, music.

Curiosity had long ceased to trouble the neighbours as to the origins of the mysterious White Cat and her household, and with the exception of crossing themselves when passing the grounds, they had given up the affair as incomprehensible. Those, however, who had seen the White Cat, said that she was a beautiful creature – her coat was like velvet and her eyes were like pearls.

One day, a knight in armour, mounted on a coal-black charger, arrived at the principal hostelry in Écija. On his shield he bore, as his coat of arms, a white cat standing on its hindlegs and, underneath, the device, 'Invincible'. Having partaken of some slight repast, he put spurs to his horse and galloped in the direction of the palace of the White Cat, but as he was never seen returning through the town, the people supposed that he must have left by some other road. The White Cat was seen the very next day walking about in the grounds, but she seemed more sorrowful than usual.

A month later, there came another knight, fully equipped and mounted on a grey charger. On his shield he also displayed a white cat, with the device, 'I win or I die'. He also galloped off to the palace, or *alcázar*, and was not seen to return, but the next day, the White Cat was more sorrowful still.

Yet another month went by, and a fresh knight appeared. He was a handsome youth, and his bearing was so manly that a crowd gathered. He was fully equipped, but on his shield he displayed a simple red cross. He partook of some food and then cantered out of town with his lance at rest.

The knight was seen to approach the palace and as soon as he thrust open the gate with his lance, a terrific roar was heard and then a sheet of fire flashed from the palace door. They all saw a horrid dragon, whose long tail, as it lashed the air, produced such a wind that it seemed as if a gale had suddenly sprung up.

The gallant knight was not daunted and eagerly searched the dragon as if to see where he might strike him. With a sudden gasp of horror, people spotted that the dragon held the White Cat under its talons, so that the Knight of the Cross when charging the dragon had to take care not to strike her. Spurring his horse on, he never pulled up till he had transfixed the dragon with his lance and, leaping out of the saddle, he drew his sword and cut off the monster's head.

No sooner had the knight chopped off the dragon's head than he was surrounded by ten enormous serpents, who all tried to coil round him, but he strangled them all with the speed of light. Then the serpents turned into twenty black vultures with fiery beaks, and they tried to peck out his eyes, but with his trusty blade he kept them off and, one by one, he killed them all.

Then the knight found himself surrounded by forty dark-haired and dark-eyed lovely maidens, who would have thrown their arms around him but, fearing their intentions were evil, he kept them at arm's length.

When looking down, he saw the White Cat there on the ground and heard her bid him to strike. He didn't hesitate but struck the maidens and cut off their heads.

No sooner had he done this than he saw that the ground was covered with burning coal, which would have scorched the White Cat and killed her had not the gallant knight lifted her to safety in his arms. He then placed her on his shield and as soon as she touched the cross she was seen transforming into a beautiful maiden and all the statues surrounding the lakes left their positions and approached her.

As soon as she could recover herself sufficiently to speak, she addressed the knight. 'Gallant knight, I am Mizpah, only daughter of Mudi Ben Raschid, who was governor of this province for many years under the Moorish King Almandázar, the Superb. My mother was the daughter of Alcharán, Governor of Mazagán, and she was a good wife and a kind mother. My father, when discovering that she had forsaken the faith of her fathers, instead embracing the religion of the Cross, so troubled her to return to her childhood's faith that she died broken-hearted.

My father then married again and his second wife, my stepmother, was a very wicked woman. She knew that I was a Christian at heart and that my lover was also a Christian, so one day, when my father was holding a banquet, she told him, 'Mudi Ben Raschid, the crescent of the Holy Prophet is waning in thy family for thy daughter is a renegade.'

My father was very much annoyed and proclaimed that he wished that his palace and his riches were made over to the enemy of mankind and that I be turned into a cat, rather than that so great a stain should fall on his family. No sooner had he finished speaking than he dropped dead and his wicked wife also, and I was turned into a cat.

My lover, Haroun, and all my young friends were turned into stone, and my servants were stricken deaf and dumb. Many a brave knight has been here to try to release me, but they all failed because they only trusted in themselves and so were defeated. But thou, gallant knight, didst trust more in the Cross than in thyself, and thou hast freed me. I am, therefore, the prize of thy good sword; deal with me as thou wilt.'

The Knight of the Cross assured her that he came from Compostela, where it was considered a duty to rescue maidens in distress and the highest reward coveted was that of doing their duty. He had, in various parts of the world, been fortunate enough to free others and he had still more work awaiting him. He trusted that the lovely Mizpah might long be spared to Haroun and, saluting her, he galloped off.

Then the wedding was held and all the good people of Écija attended. The bridegroom, rising, wished prosperity to the good knight, St James of Compostela, who had been the means of bringing about so much happiness.

BABA YAGA

Russia

Classic Russian folk tale 'Baba Yaga' is the ultimate cautionary crone story, complete with wicked stepmother. It is obviously best known for its eponymous protagonist, but as it also features a cat as a key character, it felt apt to include it in this collection. There are numerous versions of this epic tale, some longer and more elaborate.

Once upon a time, there was a man and woman who had an only daughter. When the man's wife sadly died, he took another wife. This woman, the wicked stepmother, took an instant dislike to the girl, viciously beat her and kept wondering how to be rid of the poor girl forever. One day, when the girl's father was out, the stepmother said to the girl, 'Go to your aunt, my sister, and ask her for a needle and thread to sew you a blouse.' This 'aunt' was really Baba Yaga, the bony witch.

The young girl was not stupid, and she instead went to her own aunt for advice first. 'Good morrow, Auntie,' she said. 'Mother has sent me to her sister for a needle and thread to sew me a blouse. What should I do?'

'My dear niece,' her aunt said, 'this is what you must do. You will find a birch tree there that will lash your face; you must tie it with a ribbon. You will find gates that will creak and bang; you must pour oil on the hinges. You will find dogs that will try to rip you apart; you must throw them fresh rolls. You will find a cat that will try to scratch your eyes out; you must give her some ham.'

And so the girl set off. She walked and she walked, for many miles she walked, and finally she reached the witch's abode. There was the hut, and inside it there sat Baba Yaga, the bony witch, spinning.

'Good day, Auntie,' the girl greeted her.

'Good day, dearie,' the witch replied.

'Mother sent me for a needle and thread to sew me a blouse,' said the girl.

'Very well,' Baba Yaga said, 'sit yourself down here and weave.'

The girl sat down at the loom, while Baba Yaga went out and told her maid servant, 'Go and heat up the bathhouse and give my niece a good wash; I want to eat her for breakfast.'

The maid servant did as she was told and the poor little girl was scared half to death. 'Oh, please, dear maid servant,' she begged, 'don't burn the wood, pour water on instead, and carry the water in a sieve.' And she gave the maid a piece of cloth.

While all this was going on, Baba Yaga was waiting by the window. 'Are you weaving, dear niece? Are you weaving, my dear?' she asked.

'Yes, I'm weaving, Auntie,' the girl replied. 'I'm weaving, dear aunt.'

When Baba Yaga moved away from the window, the little girl gave the cat some ham and then asked her whether there was any way to escape. 'Here is a comb and towel,' the cat replied at once. 'Take them both and run away. Baba Yaga will chase you, but if you put your ear to the ground, you will hear her coming. Then when you hear her, throw down the towel and a wide, wide river will appear. If she manages to cross the river and starts to catch you up, put your ear to the ground again and, when you hear her closing in, throw down your comb and a dense forest will appear. She will *not* be able to get through that.'

The young girl did as she was told and, grabbing the towel and comb, she ran away as fast as her little legs could carry her. As she ran from the house, the dogs tried to attack her and tear her to pieces, but she tossed them the fresh rolls and they let her pass. The gates tried to bang shut, but she poured some oil on the hinges and they let her through. The birch tree tried to lash her face, but she tied it with a ribbon and it, too, let her pass.

In the meantime, the cat sat down at the loom to weave, although, truth be told, she ended up tangling it all instead. Now and then, Baba Yaga would come to the window and call out, 'Are you weaving, dear niece? Are you weaving, my dear?'

'Yes, I'm weaving, Auntie. I'm weaving, dear aunt,' the cat would answer in a low voice.

Finally, the witch got suspicious, rushed into the hut and saw that the girl was gone. She gave the cat a good beating and scolded her severely for not scratching the girl's eyes out.

'I've served you for many years,' the cat answered her, 'yet you've never even given me a scrap of bone, but she gave me some ham.'

Baba Yaga then turned on the dogs, the gates, the birch tree and the maid servant and set to thrashing and scolding them all.

'We've served you for many years,' the dogs told her, 'yet you've never even thrown us a burnt crust, but she gave us fresh rolls.'

'We've served you for many years,' said the gates, 'yet you've never even poured water on our hinges, but she oiled them for us.'

'I've served you for many years,' said the birch tree, 'yet you've never even tied me up with thread, but she tied me with a ribbon.'

'I've served you for many years,' said the maid servant, 'yet you've never even given me a rag, but she gave me a piece of cloth.

KISA, THE CAT

Iceland

A sweet tale of redemption and sisterhood, princesses, giants and of course, cats, from the land of ice and fire.

Once upon a time, there lived a queen who had a beautiful cat the colour of smoke, with china-blue eyes, of whom she was very fond. The cat was constantly with her and followed her wherever she went, even sitting proudly by her side when she drove out in her fine glass carriage.

'Oh pussy,' said the queen one day, 'you are happier than I am, for you have a dear little kitten who is just like you, while I have nobody to play with but you.'

'Don't cry,' answered the cat, putting her paw on her mistress's arm. 'Crying never does any good. I will see what can be done.'

The cat was as good as her word. As soon as she returned from her drive, she trotted off to the forest to consult with a fairy who dwelt there, and very soon afterwards the queen had a little baby girl who seemed to be made of snow and sunbeams. The queen was delighted and soon the baby began to take notice of the little kitten as she jumped about the room and would not go to sleep at all unless the kitten lay curled up beside her.

Two or three months went by, and though the baby was still a baby, the kitten was fast becoming a cat. One evening when, as usual, the nurse came to look for her to put her in the baby's cot, she was nowhere to be found. What a search there was for that kitten, to be sure!

The servants, each anxious to find her, as the queen was certain to reward the lucky man, looked everywhere, including in the most impossible of places. Boxes that could hardly have held the kitten's paw were opened up; books were taken from bookshelves, lest the kitten should have got behind them; drawers were pulled out, for perhaps the kitten might have got shut in. But it was all to no avail. The kitten had clearly run away, and nobody could tell if it would ever choose to come back again.

Several years passed and one day, when the princess was playing ball in the garden, she happened to throw her ball farther than usual and it fell into a clump of rosebushes. The princess, of course, ran after it at once and she was stooping down to feel if it was hidden in the long grass when she heard a voice calling her.

'Ingibjörg! Ingibjörg!' it said. 'Have you forgotten me? I am Kisa, your sister.'

'But I've never *had* a sister,' Ingibjörg answered, very much puzzled for she knew nothing of what had taken place so long ago.

'Don't you remember how I always slept in your cot beside you and how you cried until I got there? Girls have no memories at all! Why, I could find my way straight up to that cot this moment if I was once inside the palace.'

'Why did you go away then?' the princess asked, but before Kisa could answer, Ingibjörg's ladies-in-waiting arrived breathless and were so horrified at the sight of a strange cat that Kisa plunged into the bushes and went back to the forest.

The princess was very much vexed with her ladies-in-waiting for frightening away her old playmate and told the queen, who came to her room every evening to bid her goodnight. 'Yes, it is quite true what Kisa told you,' the queen answered. 'I should have liked to see her again. Perhaps, some day, she will return and then you must bring her to me.'

Next morning, it was very hot and the princess declared that she must go and play in the forest, where it was always cool under the big shady trees. As usual, her minders let her do anything she pleased and sitting down on a mossy bank where a little stream flowed by, they soon fell sound asleep. The princess saw with delight that they would pay no heed to her, so she wandered on and on, expecting every moment to see some fairies dancing round a ring or some little brown elves peeping at her from behind a tree.

Alas, she met none of these – instead, a horrible giant came out of his cave and ordered her to follow him. The princess felt frightened, as he was so big and ugly, and began to feel very sorry that she had not stayed within reach of help, but as there was no use in disobeying the giant, she walked meekly behind him. They went a long, long way. Ingibjörg grew very tired and at length began to cry.

'I don't like little girls who make horrid noises,' the giant said, turning round. 'But if you *want* to cry, I will give you something to cry about.' And drawing an axe from his belt, he cut off both her feet, which he picked up and put in his pocket. Then he left.

Poor Ingibjörg lay on the grass in terrible pain, wondering if she should stay there until she died, as no one would know where to look for her. How long it was since she had set out in the morning she could not tell – it seemed like years to her, of course, but the sun was still high in the sky when she heard the sound of wheels and then, with great effort, for her throat was parched with fright and pain, she cried out for help.

'I am coming,' was the answer and a moment later, a cart driven by Kisa made its way through the trees. She was using her tail as a whip to urge the horse to go faster. As soon as Kisa saw Ingibjörg lying there, she quickly jumped down and, lifting the girl carefully in her two front paws, laid her upon some soft hay and drove back to her own little hut.

In the corner of the room was a pile of cushions and these Kisa arranged as a bed. Ingibjörg, who by this time was nearly fainting from all she had gone through, greedily drank some milk and then sank back on the cushions while Kisa fetched some dried herbs from a cupboard, soaked them in warm water and tied them on the bleeding legs. The pain vanished at once, and Ingibjörg looked up and smiled at Kisa.

'You will go to sleep now,' the cat said, 'and you will not mind if I leave you for a little while. I will lock the door and no one can hurt you.' But before she had finished, the princess was asleep.

Then Kisa got into the cart, which was standing by the door, and taking up the reins, drove straight to the giant's cave. Leaving her cart behind some trees, Kisa gently crept up to the open door and, crouching down, listened to what the giant was telling his wife, who was at supper with him.

'The first day that I can spare I shall just go back and kill her,' he was saying. 'It would never do for people in the forest to know that a mere girl can defy me.' And he and his wife were so busy calling Ingibjörg all sorts of names for her bad behaviour that they never even noticed Kisa stealing into a dark corner and upsetting a whole bag of salt into the great pot before the fire.

'Dear me, how thirsty I am!' the giant cried, by-and-by.

'So am I,' his wife answered. 'I do wish I had not taken that last spoonful of broth; I am sure something was wrong with it.'

'If I don't get some water I shall die,' the giant went on. And, rushing out of the cave, followed by his wife, he ran down the path which led to the river.

Then Kisa entered the hut and lost no time in searching every nook and cranny until she came upon some grass, under which Ingibjörg's feet were hidden and putting them in her cart, drove back again to her own hut.

Ingibjörg was grateful to see her, for she had been lying there too frightened to sleep, trembling at every noise. 'Oh, is it you?' she cried joyfully, as Kisa turned the key. And the cat came in, holding up the two neat little feet in their silver slippers.

'In two minutes, they shall be as tight as they ever were,' Kisa said, and taking some strings of the magic grass which the giant had carelessly heaped on them, she bound the feet onto the legs above. 'Of course you won't be able to walk for some time; you must not expect *that*,' she continued. 'But if you are very good, perhaps, in about a week, I may carry you home again.'

And so she did. When the cat drove the cart up to the palace gate, lashing the horse furiously with her tail, and the king and queen saw their lost daughter sitting beside her, they declared that no reward could be too great for the person who had brought her out of the giant's hands.

'We will talk about that by-and-by,' said the cat, as she made her best bow and turned her horse's head.

The princess was very unhappy when Kisa left her without even bidding her farewell. She would neither eat nor drink, nor take any notice of all the beautiful dresses her parents bought for her.

'She will die, unless we can make her laugh,' one whispered to the other. 'Is there anything in the world that we have left untried?'

'Nothing except marriage,' the king answered. He invited all the handsomest young men he could think of to the palace and bade the princess choose a husband from among them.

It took her some time to decide which one she admired the most, but at last she fixed upon a young prince whose eyes were like the pools in the forest and his hair of bright gold. The king and the queen were greatly pleased, as the young man was the son of a neighbouring king, and they gave orders that a splendid feast should be got ready.

When the marriage was over, Kisa suddenly stood before them and Ingibjörg rushed forward and clasped her in her arms. 'I have come to claim my reward,' the cat said. 'Let me sleep for this night at the foot of your bed.'

'Is that *all?*' Ingibjörg asked, much disappointed.

'It is enough,' the cat answered. And when the morning dawned, it was no cat that lay upon the bed, but a beautiful princess.

'My mother and I were both enchanted by a spiteful fairy,' Kisa said, 'and we could not free ourselves till we had carried out some kind deed that had never been done before. My mother died without ever finding a chance of doing anything new, but I took advantage of the evil act of the giant to make you as whole as ever.'

Then they were all more delighted than before and the princess lived in the court until she, too, married and went away to govern a court of her own.

THE CAT AND THE MOUSE IN A PUBLIC HOUSE

Northern Ireland

There is a good bit of humour in this tale from Northern Ireland where, for once, the mouse gets away with it, cleverly outwitting his foe, the cat.

As often happens, one night a cat was chasing a mouse, this time in a public house, and during the chase the mouse fell right into an open keg of whiskey. The mouse was drowning in the whiskey and kept crying out, 'Save me, save me!'

The cat, however, was unmoved and just told him, 'If I pull you out, it'll be to eat you.'

'Fine, I don't care,' said the mouse. 'Only get me out of here. I simply can't endure dying in booze.'

So the cat reached down the barrel and manage to paw the mouse out and put it down to play with it, but the mouse was quick. He twisted and turned, twisted and turned, until he spotted a hole nearby and, swift as a flash, the mouse sneaked into it.

'Hey, wait a minute,' said the cat. 'That's not fair play. You promised me if I pulled you out of the whiskey, you'd let me eat you!'

The mouse peeped out of the hole and squeaked back, 'Who pays any heed to what a fella says in drink?

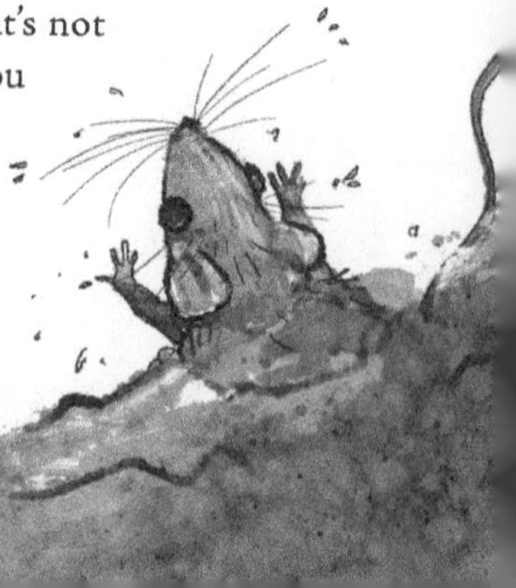

CATS IN MYTHS AND LEGENDS

Cats, big and small, appear in myths and legends across the world. Below is a quick glance at this broad topic. Some of the mythological felines will undoubtedly be familiar to you, while others may be less well known.

For cat lovers, it probably comes as no surprise that cat worship is a worldwide phenomenon, going back millennia. This chapter looks at our different feline friends – domestic and big cats – in mythology and legends. Arguably, it is big cats such as the lion, tiger or jaguar that feature more prominently in myths and legends, while the domestic cat more frequently populates the humbler folk tale. With the notable exception of Australia and New Zealand, felines in mythology can be found across the globe.

Although myths and legend have similarities with folk tales, where they differ is often in age and scope. They tend to be far older than many folk tales – going back millennia, rather than centuries or decades – and they also have wider reach. While a folk tale is often tied to a specific region or even a small village, a myth or legend may form an integral part of the whole culture of a nation or people. Myths and legends are known internationally, while the scope of the folk tale can be said to be much more local or regional.

There's an interesting polarity in feline mythology. Cats, big and small, were seen as gods or goddesses every bit as frequently as they were deemed to be demons or monsters. This 'dual nature' continues in folk tales, where cats are heroes and villains in almost equal measure.

The earliest known depictions of lions, somewhat surprisingly, hail from Europe and go back thousands of years. Lions appear in cave paintings from the Palaeolithic period (cave art between 39,000 and 15,000 years old) and are found in the Ardèche region of France and the Swabian Jura region of Germany. In Egypt, lions appear in tomb paintings from as early as 3,500 BC and they also feature in Greek, Persian, Sumerian and Mesopotamian myths, to name a few.

Africa

Arguably the most famous of mythological feline deities hail from the African continent. Egypt rivals Japan as a nation of ailurophiles, although in the case of the former, the love affair with cats is perhaps more ancient than modern. There's the Sphinx, with the body of a lion and the head of a human, and also Bastet (aka Bast), Sekhmet, Mafdet and Mut. The last four are all Egyptian goddesses associated with cats: Bastet, daughter of the sun god Ra, is usually depicted with the head of a cat and the body of a woman; Sekhmet, her sister, has the head of a lioness; protective goddess Mafdet is often depicted as a cheetah; and Mut, the mother goddess, sometimes appears as a mother cat. Furthermore, gods Kek and Maahes appear as a cat and a lion respectively. Several of these deities reflect the dual nature of cats – protection and destruction.

It is thought that through trade routes, the Egyptian love of cats spread throughout the region, influencing Middle Eastern cultures (although more recent research disputes this theory). Big cats, in particular lions, appear in Egyptian, Nubian (modern-day southern Egypt and northern Sudan), eastern and southern African mythology. The leopard appears more prominently in western and southern African cultures and mythology, while the cheetah can be found in southern African myths. Across the continent, cats, big and small, but particularly big cats, feature in many myths and legends.

The Americas

There is arguably a 'cult of the feline' across large parts of the Americas, going back hundreds, if not thousands of years. Across Mesoamerica, there are many ancient myths featuring the native big cat – the jaguar. Jaguars appear in Maya, Aztec and Olmec mythology, across the region of modern-day Mexico and parts of Central

America. *Xbalanque* and *Hunahpu*, known as the Maya Hero Twins, are sometimes depicted as were-jaguars and appear in the sacred Maya text *Popol Vuh* (first written down in the 1550s, but thought to originate much earlier).

Further south, as recently as 2020, a huge cat was found depicted at Nazca in Peru, an area famous for the so-called Nazca lines – huge 'drawings' that are best viewed from the air. This new find is thought to predate the Nazca culture, which flourished around 100 BC–AD 800. Also in Peru, the jaguar was a sacred animal to the Chavín culture in the northern Andean highlands, while the cougar (known as a puma in South America) was a sacred animal to the Inca. The Inca capital, Cusco, was laid out in the shape of a puma with the massive citadel of Sacsayhuamán representing its head. The puma is associated with power, strength and wisdom in Inca mythology.

In the United States and Canada, the lynx features in Native American and First Nation mythology, including the Ojibwa legend of *Mishipeshu*, or Great Lynx, from the area of the Great Lakes, straddling the United States–Canada border. Old Woman Moon's companion is a bobcat in Iroquois myths and it's this cat who's responsible for the waxing and waning of the moon according to one Iroquois legend.

Australasia

Although I have not come across any ancient myths or legends featuring cats from Australia or New Zealand, many parts of Asia, in particular Japan, make up for this lack. There is a wealth of myths from this nation of ailurophiles, focusing on the domestic cat, while the rest of the region includes both the mighty tiger and the lion in its myths and legends. Cats crop up time and again in Japanese folklore and folk beliefs. Consequently, it's a little challenging to determine what could be considered a folk tale and what is a myth or legend, as there is some overlap between them.

In Japanese folklore, you might come across the *kasha*, the *bakeneko*, the *nekomata*, the *gotoku neko* and *maneki-neko* – all of them slightly different versions of supernatural beings or monster cats (see glossary).

In ancient Persia, cats were seen as blessed or cursed in equal measure. Some were considered evil, or even a manifestation of the Devil himself, but they also hold an important place in Persian literature and appear in many fables. In Hebrew mythology, goddess Lilith can shapeshift and turn into a black cat; in India and Nepal, Hindu goddess Shashthi (various spellings), the protector of children, is often depicted riding a cat; goddess Parvati, also from the Hindu pantheon, is given a sacred tiger, Dawon (aka Gdon), sometimes depicted as a lion-tiger hybrid. Tigers also appear in Taiwanese, Japanese, Chinese, Korean, Thai and Vietnamese legends and myths.

Europe

From the far north, all the way to the Mediterranean, numerous different felines appear in European mythology. Europe, more than anywhere else, focuses on the humble (or not so humble) domestic cat, but the lynx also makes an appearance, particularly in Norse and Greek mythology. Iceland is home to the fearsome Yule Cat or *Jólakötturinn*, a vicious cat known to eat people at Christmas time, while in Norse mythology two cats are drawing the chariot of Norse goddess Freyja. Although they are sometimes known as Bygul and Trjegul, these two names actually have a modern source and were invented by American author Diana L. Paxson.

In Celtic mythology, *cat-sith* (Scottish Gaelic) or *cat sí* (Irish), is a fairy creature depicted as a very large, black cat with a white spot on its chest. Mostly associated with the Scottish Highlands (and possibly inspired by the Scottish wildcat), there are many myths and legends featuring *cat-sith* in Scottish folklore, with some appearing in Ireland as well. Sometimes, this spectral cat is depicted as a witch who has the ability to transform into a cat nine times, in others, it was believed to be a demon disguised as cat. Folk belief held that *cat-sith* would steal the souls of the recently deceased and so people would hold wakes to ensure the cat would not be able to get its paws on the dearly departed. In nearby Wales, *cath palug* is a monster cat in the Arthurian legend. While many cats did not fare so well in the Middle Ages, the medieval King of Wales, *Hywel Dda* (Good), made it illegal to kill or harm a cat.

Down south, in Galicia, in the north-western corner of Spain, the creature known as *Gatipedro* is rather unusual. This large, white cat with a brown horn on its head is known for his sneaky behaviour – he enters children's bedrooms at night, pours water through his horn, making the sleeping children dream they're bed-wetting and thus causing them to actually wet their beds. Not perhaps the scariest of monsters, this kitty seems more annoying than anything else. In some

tales of Galician folklore, *Gatipedro* only turns up on certain nights, for example, when there's a full moon; in other tales, *Gatipedro* only visits those children that have been naughty during the day.

Southern France, Gascony and Brittany are populated by the mythical 'magician cat', *matagot* (or *mandagot*), generally depicted as a black cat, but sometimes as another animal. The *matagots* are thought to be evil spirits in animal form, but if well looked after and fed, they can bring good luck and wealth to a household.

The above is just a small snapshot of the many different cats that appear in myths and legends from across the globe.*

* Numerous sources were used for this chapter, including: Espsäter, A.M., *Cats: A Miscellany* (Summersdale, 2015); de Caro, F. (ed.) & K. Harvill (illustrator), *The Folktale Cat* (August House Inc., 1993); Briggs, K.M., *Nine Lives: Cats in Folklore* (Routledge & Kegan Paul, 1980); Marshall, B.C., (translated and retold) & K. Van Deusen (ed.), *Far North Tales: Stories from the Peoples of the Arctic Circle* (Libraries Unlimited, ABC-CLIO, LLC, 2011). Online sources: www.catster.com; en.wikipedia.org; www.largehope.com; www.peopleforanimalsindia.org; www.petinsurance.co.za; www.fabulahub.com; www.iranicaonline.org; www.meigasgallegas.com; www.bbc.co.uk/news/world-latin-america-54593295

SUPERSTITIONS SAYINGS AND SHIPS' CATS

Cats have formed an integral part of global culture for centuries, so it's hardly surprising that they are associated with all sorts of folk beliefs and superstitions. In the English language, cats crop up in multiple sayings and phrases, some ancient, some more modern. This chapter looks at some of these beliefs and sayings, as well as the important role played by ships' cats.

Cats are often thought to embody quite opposite traits and this is reflected in superstitions, folklore and folk beliefs, even sayings and proverbs. Our feline friends have, in different eras and different parts of the world, been deemed good or bad luck, good or bad omens in equal measure. They've been seen as witches' familiars, shapeshifters, demons, gods and goddesses, werecats and monster cats.

Superstitions associated with cats are numerous throughout the world and cats are often believed to have supernatural or magical powers. While some of these beliefs go back centuries, even millennia, others are more modern. From harbingers of death to predicting the weather, there are so many superstitions associated with felines that this chapter is only able to scratch and claw at the surface of this vast topic.

Cats also crop up in many phrases and sayings – and not just in English, although I'm limiting myself to those in the English language here. Below are some of the most prevalent superstitions and folk beliefs about cats, a glance at the history of some of our best-known 'cat sayings' and the importance of ships' cats, including some famous 'shipping felines'.

SUPERSTITIONS

Black cats do not fare well when it comes to superstitions. Many of the beliefs associated with black felines seem to date back to the Middle Ages, when cats in general had a tough time. They were thought to be witches' familiars, aiding and protecting them when doing the Devil's work. Witches were also believed to be able to shapeshift and turn into their familiars, usually a cat or a raven.

Another prevalent superstition was that the Devil himself would turn into a black cat to socialise with the witches in league with him, or that the black cat was a demon in disguise. These superstitions appear to have been widespread across Europe and beyond at certain times in history.

In the United Kingdom and Italy, a cat sneezing is said to bring good luck to the whole household – unless it sneezes three times. Then you will catch a cold (perhaps from the cat?).

Cats are believed to not only be able to predict the weather, but also to predict earthquakes. As animals in general tend to sense earthquakes before humans, there is probably some truth in this belief. There are many weather myths associated with cats in the United Kingdom and elsewhere. A cat snoring was said to mean foul weather was coming; a cat sitting with its back to the open fire meant warmer weather was on its way; and a cat washing its ears would mean rain was approaching.

In Russia, seeing a blue cat (the Russian blue, presumably) is thought to be good luck, while more disturbingly, over in Czechia, burying a cat in a field is said to bring a good harvest.

In ancient Egypt, cats were believed to have the power to ward off evil spirits – quite the opposite to Europe where, for several centuries, cats were believed to be evil spirits themselves. In fact, throughout northern Africa – Morocco, Algeria, Tunisia – cats are seen as sacred animals and protectors of the household. This holds true across the Islamic countries. In West Africa, by contrast (particularly in Yoruba culture), cats were traditionally seen as a bad omen, associated with witchcraft and the supernatural.

Mystical cat superstitions from Japan perfectly portray the duality of feline myths. Cats are viewed as both symbols of good luck and bad luck, with a slight emphasis on 'monster-cats' as opposed to 'fortune cats'. Most famous of all internationally is *Maneki-neko,* the beckoning cat that can be found in shops and other establishments and is believed to bring good luck and fortune. *Maneki-neko,* however, has plenty of more gruesome monster-cat counterparts, such as the *bakeneko, nekomata* and *kasha.*

SAYINGS

The English language is liberally sprinkled with expressions, phrases and sayings featuring felines. Who hasn't heard of 'the cat's whiskers', read about 'fatcats' in the media, been called a 'scaredy cat' or a 'copycat'? Cats populate so many sayings that we barely stop to ask ourselves where they all hail from and how they came to gracefully saunter into our everyday vocabulary, with a 'swish and flick' of the tail. Below is an attempt at explaining some of the most common expressions and sayings in modern-day English usage.

Cats Have Nine Lives

Perhaps the most enduring myth about cats is that they have nine lives. Although agile and resilient, cats, sadly, do not possess multiple lives. The origins of this belief remain unclear, but there is evidence that it goes back centuries and might be rooted in ancient Egyptian, Greek or Arabic culture. The number nine appears in both Greek and Norse mythology. Interestingly, in English-speaking countries, cats are said to have nine lives, while in Spanish they 'only' have seven and in the Arab world, six. There is an English proverb that states, 'A cat has nine lives, for three he plays, for three he strays, and for the last three he stays'.

'Cat Got Your Tongue?'

The origins of this phrase are somewhat hazy … It's been suggested that it hails from a time when kings used to punish their subjects by cutting out their tongues and feeding them to the resident cats, but this appears to be a myth. It's more likely to be a reference to a cat o' nine tails, a whip used to flog disobedient sailors of the British Royal Navy and so it literally meant you'd been flogged into silence. That said, there is a tale of feeding your enemies' tongues to the cats, which hails from ancient Egypt where cats were revered.

Letting the Cat Out of the Bag

There are various theories about the origins of the saying 'to let the cat out of the bag', in other words, to reveal a secret or hidden information, whether deliberately or, more commonly, by mistake. The most plausible dates back as far as 1530 and refers to cats being substituted for piglets at the market. If the cat was let out of the bag, the trickery would be exposed and you would be able to avoid buying 'pigs in a poke' (a 'poke' is a type of bag). In German and Dutch, there's a similar phrase which refers to buying false goods. Another theory is that cats in the Middle Ages were released from a bag into barns and other areas with a rat problem. However, this doesn't really explain the meaning of the phrase.

There's More Than One Way to Skin a Cat

An alternative version of this rather gruesome expression, meaning there's more than one way of achieving a goal, dates back to a 1678 version of English proverbs, while the current phrase first appears in writing in 1840. By then, it seems to be in common usage and readily understood by the reading public. Its origins are somewhat hazy, but it is believed the phrase was originally taken quite literally, as cat fur was a cheap alternative to more luxurious furs and was used for coats and other garments. The use of cat fur is mentioned in a thirteenth-century text for nuns and the cats were usually skinned alive. Over the centuries the meaning shifted and by the 1800s, the phrase had taken on the meaning it has today.

The Cat's Whiskers

This phrase, meaning something outstanding or the best of something – 'the bee's knees', to quote another phrase – is more modern in origin and first shows up in writing in the United States in the early 1920s. This type of slang, to denote something exceptionally good, appears to have been widely used Stateside by the late 1920s.

Curiosity Killed the Cat

Highlighting the dangers of being too nosy or inquisitive, this proverb dates back several centuries in its original form, 'care killed the cat', and was even mentioned by Shakespeare in the 1590s. The more modern version, 'curiosity killed the cat' was in use by the 1860s, although its transition from 'care' (meaning 'worry') to 'curiosity' is unclear. The phrase crops up in numerous books, including Stephen King's 1977 horror novel, *The Shining.*

Looks Like Something the Cat Brought or Dragged in

Another slang term with origins across 'the pond', this American-English phrase dates to at least the late 1800s. Initially, the word 'bring', rather than 'dragged', was used. It could be said to mean what it says on the tin – to look bedraggled, dishevelled and somewhat disgusting – like something the cat has caught, killed and dragged in.

Raining Cats and Dogs

An expression that means 'to rain very heavily', there are many theories of its origins. In seventeenth-century Europe, many stray cats and dogs died in the streets and due to the poor drainage systems they'd be left littering the streets after downpours, making it look like the rain had brought them. In the United Kingdom, during the Tudor era, animals were often kept in the rafters below the roof and heavy rains could bring them to the ground level of houses and cottages. Sailors at sea would refer to heavy winds as 'dogs' and lots of rain as 'cats', potentially coining the phrase 'it's raining cats and dogs'. These are just some of numerous theories, but the origins of the phrase remain shrouded in mystery.

No Room to Swing a Cat

Meaning a very confined space, this expression likely refers to the cat o' nine tails whip and the difficulty of swinging it on the deck of a ship. This rather nasty tool for punishing misdemeanours was used onboard British Royal Navy ships. But there is also an older and no less gruesome explanation for the phrase, which dates to the sixteenth century, when cats were swung as target practice.

Put/Throw/Set the Cat Among the Pigeons

This British idiom, meaning to say or do something that will cause trouble or controversy, dates from the early 1700s. There are some reports that it referred to a man entering into the company of a group of women, while others contend that it literally referred to putting a cat in a pigeon pen. The meaning has expanded and shifted over the centuries and there are many similar sayings in different parts of the world – for example, 'let a goat into the garden' in Russian, 'disturb the dovecote' in Spanish. The Grand Dame of crime, Agatha Christie, wrote a murder mystery entitled *Cat Among the Pigeons* in 1959.

While/When the Cat's Away (the Mice Will Play)

This proverb, meaning people will often naturally take advantage of the absence of authority figures and behave badly, was popularised in the 1600s, although its actual origins are hazy. It appears in writing as early as 1470, and Shakespeare includes it in his play *Henry the Fifth*. There are Spanish, French, German and Russian versions of the proverb, to name a few. The notion that when there is no authority in place people will do as they please seems to be a deep-held belief right across the globe.

SHIPS' CATS

There are many superstitions and, as evidenced above, several sayings associated with seafaring and ships' cats. It was ships' cats sailing the seven seas that first brought felines to many different parts of the world, including the Americas, Australia and New Zealand. They are featured in some of our best-known and best-loved feline folk tales, such as 'Dick Whittington and His Cat', and Dick Whittington's story is mirrored by the Danish folk tale, 'The House of Katholm' (see European section, pages 112 and 140), although the cat in the Danish tale remains nameless.

In times gone by, ships' cats were essential to keep precious cargo safe from mice and other rodents on long sea voyages – they provided much-needed pest control. There is archaeological evidence that Egyptian cats travelled along Mediterranean trade routes as early as the eighth century BC. The Vikings also kept cats onboard their ships, and later, during the age of exploration and colonisation (the fifteenth to eighteenth centuries), cats were able to reach all corners of the globe, including the regions with no previous feline population such as Oceania.

Times have changed, though, and since 1975, cats are banned from Royal Navy ships, although they remain popular onboard private vessels. Cats were thought to be lucky animals to have onboard ship and there are tales of captains or crew refusing to sail without a cat onboard. They were believed to be able to predict the weather or have magical powers. Polydactyl cats (ones with extra toes) were thought to be the luckiest of all by some sailors and these became particularly well known as ships' cats.

In Yorkshire, in the United Kingdom, sailors' or fishermen's wives kept black cats at home to ensure their husbands' safe return. Cats were thought to be able to both raise storms and protect a ship in foul weather. Should a cat fall overboard, it was quickly rescued, as it was feared that it would otherwise summon up a terrible storm. If the ship survived the storm, it would still be cursed with nine years of bad luck if the cat perished.

Over the centuries, many ships' cats, have become famous felines in their own right and this is particularly true after the Second World War, when both US and British Royal Navy ships kept cats onboard. One such kitty, called Blackie, sailed with Winston Churchill onboard HMS *Prince of Wales* from Britain to Canada in 1941. Having met the man himself, Blackie was then renamed Churchill in his honour. He survived the sinking of HMS *Prince of Wales*, later that year, and arrived in Singapore with the other survivors. His fate afterwards is shrouded in mystery, and one can only hope he found a good home with plenty of fresh fish after all his adventures.

Another well-travelled, modern-day cat, was Chibley, who circumnavigated the globe five times before passing away in Lunenburg, Nova Scotia, Canada, in 2011. Also in Canada, in 1921, Ada Blackjack, a young Inuit woman, survived the wilds of the Arctic together with Vic, the cat who kept her company in the subzero temperatures. She was rescued two years later.

There are many other well-documented ships' cats, too numerous to mention here. Some have had their seafaring adventures documented in books or even films. There was Mrs Chippy, who travelled onboard Shackleton's ship, *Endurance*, and Unsinkable Sam, a ship's cat on no less than three ships that were all torpedoed in the Second World War. If you need proof of a cat's resilience, adaptability and courage, look no further than the hardy ship's cat.*

* Numerous sources, including de Caro, F. (ed.), & K. Harvill (illustrator), *The Folktale Cat* (August House Inc., 1993); Briggs, K.M., *Nine Lives: Cats in Folklore* (Routledge & Kegan Paul, 1980); Webster, R., *The Encyclopedia of Superstitions* (Llewellyn Publications, 2008); online sources: www.seahistory.org; www.allthatsinteresting.com; www.phrases.org.uk; www.grammarist.com; www.wordhistories.net; www.en.wikipedia.org; www.catster.com; www.thehistoryofenglish.com

EPILOGUE

I'll leave you with this short tale that I felt inspired to pen after my months of feline folk tale research. Welcome to the Village of Thunderous Purrs, home to pussycats of all cat-kinds.

THE VILLAGE OF THUNDEROUS PURRS

In the Village of Thunderous Purrs there have lived many a feline throughout the ages and many live there still. Five of these village felines – Friendly-cat, 'Fraidy-cat, Fluffy-cat, Fearsome-cat and Funny-cat – were particularly close to each other.

It often happened that on dark and stormy nights, they all gathered together to curl up by a blazing open fire and tell each other tales, some taller than others. For, as I'm sure you must know, just as folks get together to tell folk tales, cats come together to tell cat tales.

Friendly-cat, who thought very highly of the art of friendship and excellent camaraderie, would usually get the storytelling off to a good start. This evening, she began by gently purring the tale of the four cats who were going to become town musicians in Bremen (because in cat tales, *all* the protagonists are, of course, feline). She would spellbind her captive kitty audience with this wonderful tale of how the elderly, stalwart friends manage to outsmart a band of robbers and get their very own retirement home into the bargain.

Next up was 'Fraidy-cat, who, in all honesty, was a little scared of the world and everything and everyone in it. That said, 'Fraidy-cat really wanted to believe that humans could be sweet and kind, even if he had not been lucky enough to encounter many such humans himself. Thus, he meowed, rather plaintively, the lovely tale of the Prophet Muhammad, who'd treated his cat Muezza and all other cats with such gentle kindness and care.

Then it was Fluffy-cat's turn, and she was truly the spoilt, precious princess puss of the lot. Most of the time, she just sat admiring herself in front of the mirror or perhaps grooming her gloriously shiny fur, but once in a while, she could be prevailed upon to join the storytelling circle and tell a tale. As she loved beautiful protagonists, a bit of adventure *and* a happy ending, Fluffy-cat chose to loudly purr and, if a particular part of the tale warranted it, hiss the romantic tale of the cats' elopement. At least in the cat world, star-crossed lovers got a happier ending than Romeo and Juliet, leaving all the cats purring in contentment.

All except Fearsome-cat, that is. He was quite the fiercest and most ferocious of this band of feline friends, and unsurprisingly, he chose to tell a monster-cat story. You see, Fearsome-cat wasn't quite content to be just a cat. No, he had tiger ambitions, and he thought, surely, if he stood tall, fur and tail raised, teeth bared, he did indeed look rather like a tiger. And this is how he delivered the tale of the Tiger Aunt who comes to eat little children. He yowled and howled and growled his way through the horror story until all his kitty friends were cowering in fright, hiding under tables and chairs. Oh, how they wished Fearsome-cat wouldn't be quite so *dramatic*, acting everything out with wild abandon. He really did take himself rather too seriously, they all thought.

Luckily, at the end of the evening, Funny-cat could be relied upon to lighten the mood for everyone, miaowing the humorous tale of the little old lady who was granted three wishes, but still ended up feeling sorely disappointed. All the cats chuckled heartily at that one, especially the male cats, even if they also empathised with their story counterpart.

The stories continued late into the night, as felines do like a good night-time ramble. The five of them, who have been telling cat tales for many moons gone by, will undoubtedly be telling ever more such tales for many moons to come.

And cat tales do travel ... They may have been meowed, miaowed, yowled, howled, growled, purred or hissed over the years, wandering from kitty to kitty. Some tales have travelled from rooftop to garden to backyard or even crossed oceans with ships' cats. Other tales have been read to domestic moggies by the humble servants that serve their beloved cats' needs to the best of their ability.

If you listen carefully, you may find, to your surprise, that like the five felines in this story, your cats are re-miaowing some of the feline folk tales found in this very book.

GLOSSARY

Alcázar	A palace or fortress of Moorish origin.
Alderman	A member of local government or other high-ranking official in the United Kingdom, in the past.
Bakeneko	A monster or ghost cat with shapeshifting abilities in Japanese folklore.
Cath Palug	A monstrous cat from Welsh mythology, associated with Arthurian legends.
Cat-sith/sí	A creature from Celtic mythology, often appearing as a large, black cat.
Gatipedro	A legendary creature from Galician folklore, often depicted as a white cat with a brown horn on its forehead.
Gaucho	A cowboy from the Pampas region of South America.
Gotoku neko	A type of *nekomata* (see below) in Japanese folklore, often depicted with two tails.
Hâfiz	A person who has memorised the entire Koran by heart.
Hajji	A Muslim who has been to Mecca as a pilgrim.
Hombre Gato (El)	A shapeshifting being, capable of transforming from a man into a large, black cat. A popular myth in rural Argentina.
Hóo-Koo-Pô	The Tiger Aunt in Taiwanese folk tales.
Kasha	A monster-cat in Japanese folklore, known for stealing corpses.
Koto	A Japanese zither.
Mainá	'Bird' or 'Songbird' in Hindi.
Maneki-neko	Known as the Lucky or Beckoning cat in Japanese folklore.
Matagot/ Mandagot	A spirit from French folklore that takes the shape of a black cat.
Muezza	The name of the Prophet Muhammad's cat.
Nekomata	Cat *yōkai* from Japanese folklore, usually depicted with a forked tail; there are mountain or domestic versions.
O pulo do gato	A popular Brazilian saying, meaning to have something up one's sleeve or not give away all one's secret tricks
Pampas	Fertile grassland that stretches across parts of Argentina, Uruguay and southern Brazil.

Schadenfreude	Enjoying someone else's misfortune.
Shader	Shadow.
Tangará	A colourful bird native to parts of South America.
Yōkai	Shapeshifting beings or spirits with supernatural powers in Japanese folklore.

SOURCES

Most tales have been freely adapted and, in some cases, also translated by the author.

Feline Folk Tales – Africa

The Obstinate Child – Basset, R., *Moorish Literature* (London & New York: The Colonial Press, 1901).

The Cat Who Came Indoors – Eastern/Swahili and southern African oral folk tale. There are many different versions in print, including Nelson Mandela's *Favorite African Folk Tales* (W.W. Norton & Co., illustrated edition, 2008).

The Cats and the Mice – Oral folk tale from Wollega (also spelled Welega), Ethiopia. Adapted from www.ethiopianfolktales.com

The Tortoise and His Debts – Cobham, H., 'Animal Stories from Calabar', *Journal of the Royal African Society*, 1905.

The Wildcat and the Gazelle – Dennett, R.E., 'Notes on the Folklore of the Fjort', publisher for the Folk-lore Society (London, 1898).

The Wildcat and the Nightjar – Kaonde oral folk tale from Zambia. Freely adapted from Ganly, J.C., *Kaonde Proverbs* (Zambia: Ndola Mission Press, 1987).

The Wildcat and the Monkey – Ellis, A.B., *The E'we-Speaking Peoples of the Slave Coast of West Africa* (London: Chapman & Hall Ltd, 1890).

The Cat and the Leopard (aka Why the Leopard Can Only Catch Prey on Its Left Side) – Barker, W.H., & C. Sinclair, *West African Folk Tales* (United Kingdom: George G. Harrap & Co., 1917).

Nunda, the Eater of People – Steere, E., *Swahili Tales* (London: Bell & Daldy, 1870).

Feline Folk Tales – The Americas

Wildcat Gets a New Face – Alden Mason, J., 'Myths of the Uintah Utes', *Journal of American Folklore*, 1910.

The Dance of the *Tangarás* – Brazilian oral folk tale, retold by storyteller Fabio Sombra, Rio de Janeiro, Brazil: fabiosombrapainter.blogspot.com/

Lion Brooks No Rival – Bacon, A.M., & E.C. Parsons, 'Folk-Lore from Elizabeth City County, Virginia', *The Journal of American Folk-Lore*, Vol. 35, No. 137 (July–September 1922). Original storyteller: William Franklin of Montgomery County, Alabama.

Why are Cats So Arrogant? – Brazilian version of 'The Cat Who Came Indoors', retold by storyteller Fabio Sombra, Rio de Janeiro, Brazil: fabiosombrapainter.blogspot.com

Cactus Cat – Mexican oral folk tale, adapted from online sources: https://abookofcreatures.com/2019/09/20/cactus-cat/ and https://fantasia-y-mitologia.fandom.com/es/wiki/Gato_Cactus

The Lynx Who Ate Himself – Adapted from The Native American Article Archives: www.bigorrin.org/archives.htm. Also published in *Far North Tales: Stories From the Peoples of the Arctic Circle*, translated and retold by B.C. Marshall and edited by K. Van Deusen, (Libraries Unlimited, ABC-CLIO, LLC, 2011).

El Hombre Gato – Oral folk tale from rural Argentina, numerous sources, including en.wikipedia.org/wiki/Hombre_Gato

Wait Until Emmett Comes – Oral folk tale from southern United States (other versions from West Virginia). Retold by storyteller Amelia Ace Armande from Ropetackle Storytellers, United Kingdom https://linktr.ee/ropetacklestorytellers.

The Cat, the Dog and Death – Courlander, H., *The Piece of Fire and Other Haitian Tales* (New York: Harcourt, 1964).

Why Dogs Chase Cats – Oral African-American folk tale, numerous versions in print, including *Why Dogs Chase Cats* by O. Bala (Booksbybalas, 2021).

The Cat's Leap – Brazilian oral folk tale, retold by storyteller Fabio Sombra, Rio de Janeiro, Brazil fabiosombrapainter.blogspot.com/

Three Wishes – There are several versions of this tale. This one has been freely adapted from an oral tale from Indiana, United States.

Feline Folk Tales – Australasia

Prophet Muhammad's Cat – Oral tale from the Middle East. Many versions exist in print, including www.thegreatcat.org/history-of-the-cat-in-the-dark-ages-part-6/

The Lion and the Hare – The Panchatantra, Book 1, India. The Panchatantra (also spelled Pañcatantra or Pañca-tantra) consists of five books of animal fables and magic tales (some eighty-seven stories in all), which were compiled in their current form between the third and fifth centuries AD sites.pitt.edu/~dash/type0092.html#panchatantra

Why Dogs Wag Their Tails – Cook Cole, M., *Philippine Folk Tales* (A.C. McClurg & Co., 1916).

Maneki-neko, the Beckoning Cat – Japanese folk tale from the Edo period (seventeenth to mid-nineteenth centuries), many versions exist. The story included here is freely adapted from a variety of sources.

The Cat as Holy Man – Hanauer J.E., *Folk-Lore of the Holy Land: Moslem, Christian, and Jewish*, edited by M. Pickthall (London: Duckworth & Company, 1907).

Hóo-Koo-Pô, the Tiger Aunt – Many written versions exist, including Yep, L., *Auntie Tiger* (HarperCollins, 2009). The story dates back to the sixteenth century.

The Boy Who Drew Cats – Hearn, L. (translator), *Japanese Fairy Tales: The Boy Who Drew Cats* (Tokyo: T. Hasegawa, 1898).

The Phantom Big Cats of Australia – Numerous online sources and newspaper clippings, including: www.reddit.com/r/UnresolvedMysteries/comments/nf7s66/the_mystery_of_australias_phantom_cats/?rdt=32944; www.news.com.au/technology/science/animals/the-grisly-mystery-of-the-murderous-tantanoola-tiger/news-story/ac9051acbddebcb9baf850f70501d095; www.reddit.com/r/UnresolvedMysteries/comments/nf7s66/the_mystery_of_australias_phantom_cats/?rdt=32944; www.reddit.com/r/UnresolvedMysteries/comments/nf7s66/the_mystery_of_australias_phantom_cats/?rdt=32944

Why Dog and Cat are Enemies – Wilhelm, Dr R., *The Chinese Fairy Book* (New York: Frederick A. Stokes Company, 1921).

The Vampire Cat of Nabéshima – Mitford, A.B., *Tales of Old Japan* (London: Macmillan, 1871).

The Two Cats – Tibbitts, C.J., *Folk-lore and Legends: Oriental* (London: W.W. Gibbings, 1889).

Old Mountain Uncle, the Tiger Without Manners – Griffis, W. E., *The Unmannerly Tiger, and Other Korean Tales* (New York: Thomas Y. Crowell Co., 1911).

The Cat and the Mice – O'Connor W.F., *Folk Tales from Tibet* (London: Hurst & Blackett Ltd, 1906).

The Baldheaded Cat of Kowashi – Suzuki, Y., *Japanese Legends and Folk-Tales* (Tokyo, Japan: Sakuri Shoten, 1949).

The Tiger and the Shadow and The King of the Tigers is Sick – Skeat, W., *Fables and Folk-Tales from an Eastern Forest* (Cambridge University Press, 1901).

The Cat Which Could Not be Killed – 'Indian Fairy Tales, 1880' told by Dunkní at Simla, 26 July 1876, collected and translated by Maive Stokes, 1880.

The Cats' Elopement – Lang, A., *The Pink Fairy Book* (London: Longmans, Green & Co., 1897).

Kasha: the Japanese Fire cat –en.wikipedia.org/wiki/Kasha_(folklore); yokai.com/; yjapanesemythicalcreatures.com/creatures/kasha.php; Davisson, Z., *KAIBYŌ: The Supernatural Cats of Japan (Chin Music Press Inc., 2017)*; Sekien, T., *Illustrated Demon Horde's Night Parade* (Japan: 1776)

Feline Folk Tales – Europe

Dick Whittington and His Cat – Jacobs, J., *English Fairy Tales* (David Nutt, 1890) and many other versions.

When the Governor's Cat Set Fire to the City of Umeå – Gustavsson, P., *Sägenresan, Fantastiska Berättelser från Skåne till Lappland* (Stockholm: Rabén & Sjögren, 2006. From Sägenresan digital map with kind permission from the Museum of Legends (sagenresan.sagobygden.se/)

The Heron, the Cat and the Bramble – Oral history interview in Welsh, with Lewis T. Evans (1882–1975) on 13 April 1968 (Recording No. AV 1845; interviewer: Robin Gwyndaf). He heard this story from his uncle, Lewis Evans, Hafod Llan Isa, Pentrellyncymer, from the book *Y Meudwy Cymreig Ffynhonnell Storiau*: museum.wales/collections/folktales/?story=32

The Cat and the Mouse Set Up House – Grimm, J. & W., *'Katze und Maus in Gesellschaft' in Kinder- und Hausmärchen* (Children's and Household Tales), *Grimms' Fairy Tales* No. 2. Translated by Margaret Hunt (1884).

The Legend of the Pussy Willow – Based on an oral folk tale from Poland, numerous versions available (from different parts of Europe, as well as North America).

King o' the Cats – Jacobs, J., *More English Fairy Tales* (London: David Nutt Publisher, 1894).

The Kitty on Dovrefjell Mountain – Peter Christen Asbjørnsen and Jørgen Moe, '*Kjetta på Dovre*', *Norske Folkeeventyr* (1852). 'The Cat on the Dovrefell', *Popular Tales from the Norse*, 2nd edition, translated by George Webbe Dasent (Edinburgh: Edmonston and Douglas, 1859), pp. 103–04.

The Cat, the Cock and the Fox – Nisbet Bain, R. (ed. and trans.), *Cossack Fairy Tales and Folk Tales* (London: George G. Harrap & Co., 1916).

The Clever Kitty – (With kind permission from Bengt af Klintberg) Af Klintberg, B., *Svenska Sagor och Sägner vol. 13, Sagor från Bohuslän*, Kungliga Gustav Adolfs Akademien för svensk folkkultur, Uppsala 2022 (storyteller, August Jakobsson from Tanum)

Why the Manx Cat has No Tail – Original folk tale-inspired story provided for this collection by storyteller David Thompson from Texas, United States.

The Bremen Town Musicians – Grimm J. & W., '*Die Bremer Stadtmusikanten*', *Kinder- und Hausmärchen gesammelt durch die Brüder Grimm*, 7th edition (Göttingen: Verlag der Dieterichschen Buchhandlung, 1857), No. 27, pp. 145–48. The Grimms' source: Dorothea Viehmann (1755–1815). The Grimms first published this tale in the second edition of their *Kinder- und Hausmärchen* (1819).

The House of Katholm – Tibbitts,C.J., *Folk-lore and Legends Scandinavia* (London: W.W. Gibbings, 1890).

King Cat – Adapted from Ortutay, G. (ed.), *Hungarian Folk Tales* (Budapest: Corvina, 1962).

The Dog, the Cat and the Mouse – Gaster, M., *Rumanian Bird and Beast Stories* (London: Folk-Lore Society, 1915).

The Death of Kasserikus – Af Klintberg, B., *Svenska folksägner* (Stockholm, 1998 [1972]); Gustavsson, P., *Läskiga vidunder och sällsamma djur* (Stockholm, 2008). From Sägenresan digital map with kind permission from the Museum of Legends (sagenresan.sagobygden.se/).

The White Cat of Écija – Sellers C., *Tales from the Lands of Nuts and Grapes* (London: Field & Tuer et al., 1888).

Baba Yaga – Oral Russian folk tale, many versions exist. Afanas'ev, A., *Russian Fairy Tales* (8 volumes, published from 1855–67).

Kisa, the Cat – Lang, A., *The Brown Fairy Book* (1904).

The Cat and the Mouse in a Public House – Murphy, M.J., *Now You're Talking: Folk Tales from the North of Ireland* (Belfast: Blackstaff Press Ltd, 1975).

BIBLIOGRAPHY

Briggs, K.M., *Nine Lives: Cats in Folklore* (Routledge & Kegan Paul, 1980).

de Caro, F. (ed.), & K. Harvill (illustrator), *The Folktale Cat* (August House Inc., 1993).

Castle, P., *Where Dragons Soar and Other Animal Folk Tales of the British Isles* (The History Press, 2016).

Engh, S-E., *Danish Folk Tales* (The History Press, 2023).

Espsäter, A.M., *Cats: A Miscellany* (Summersdale, 2015).

Far North Tales: Stories From the Peoples of the Arctic Circle, translated and retold by B.C. Marshall, edited by K. Van Deusen (Libraries Unlimited, ABC-CLIO, LLC, 2011).

Hellberg Moberg, A.M.V., *Swedish Folk Tales* (illustrated by R. Day) (The History Press, 2024).

Koskimies, A.V., & T.I. Itkonen (revised by L. Laitinen, edited and translated by T. Frandy) *Inari Sámi Folklore – Stories from Aanaar* (The University Press of Wisconsin, 2019).

Nordic Folk Tales, illustrations by U. Thynell (Chronicle Books, 2019).

Pullman, P., *Grimm Tales for Young and Old* (Penguin Classics, 2012).

Schneidau, L., *Botanical Folk Tales of Britain and Ireland* (The History Press, 2018)

Stefánsson, H.H., *Icelandic Folk Tales* (illustrated by T. Sandström Fahlström) (The History Press, 2020).

Swedish Folk Tales, illustrated by J. Bauer (Floris Books, 2004).

Webster, R., *The Encyclopedia of Superstitions* (Llewellyn Publications, 2008).

Archives

Institute for Language and Folklore (ISOF) Archives: www.isof.se/

Land of Legends and Museum of Legends Archives: sagobygden.se/

ACKNOWLEDGEMENTS

Many people from different parts of the world have had a hand in the creation of this book – cat lovers, storytellers, writers, friends, friends of friends and furry, four-legged friends …

First of all, I'd like to thank Nicola Guy and everyone at The History Press, who, I'm pleased to say, liked the idea when I approached them with my *Feline Folk Tales* book proposal in the autumn of 2024.

Very special thanks to the Society of Authors (societyofauthors.org) and the Authors' Foundation for awarding me a grant that facilitated the research and allowed me time to focus on completing this book.

Fabio Sombra, a storyteller, artist and writer from Rio de Janeiro in Brazil, deserves a special mention for contributing three stories (and a 'bonus recipe' for *pão de queijo* bread into the bargain) https://fabiosombrapainter.blogspot.com/. Also special thanks to Ben Box, who put me in touch with Fabio in the first place, as well as sending lots of interesting research on Latin American folk tales and mythology my way.

Thanks/*Diolch yn fawr* to Sally Donovan and Grace Todd from Museum Wales/*Amgueddfa Cymru* in Cardiff.

Thanks also to Orcadian storyteller, Tom Muir (www.orkneyology.com/), who pointed me in the direction of several cat tales, including the Shetland Islands' version of the Brothers Grimm tale 'The Cat and the Mouse Set up House'; storyteller and author Pete Castle (https://petecastle.co.uk/pete-castle/); storyteller and actor Amelia Ace Armande from Ropetackle Storytellers (https://linktr.ee/ropetacklestorytellers); Vanessa Woolf from Connection with Wonder (https://connectionwithwonder.com/), all in the UK; and storyteller David Thompson in Texas, United States.

Among the cat lovers, I'd like to thank Tine Winther and Lotta Welmsö from the Land of Legends in Sweden (https://sagobygden.se/en/) and Victoria and Beki from the Love Cats Agency in London (https://love-cats.uk/) and all the fabulous felines – from ancient mythological deities to happily-sitting-on-my-lap-in-everyday-life moggies – who have come into my life these last twenty years.

Also special thanks to my partner and friends, who have been very patient while I've been compiling this book. And extra-special thanks to the Bowie-cat for all the purring!

ABOUT THE AUTHOR

Anna Maria Vilhelmina Hellberg Moberg is a UK-based writer, storyteller, journalist and cat lover, originally from rural Värmland in western Sweden. She spent over a decade as a travel writer and is the author of more than twenty-five books, as well as numerous features for the British and international press. Her works include travel and culinary books focusing on Scandinavia and Latin America, a fairy tale for adults, two collections of short stories, the travel memoir *Wayward Wanderings*, three books about cats (fiction and creative non-fiction) and, most recently, a book of Swedish folk tales (The History Press, 2024).

Her poetry has been published in Swedish and English and her photography has been exhibited in Sweden and the United Kingdom. As a storyteller, she tells folk and fairy tales, autobiographical and fictitious tales as Vilhelmina/ A.M.V. Hellberg Moberg.

In the United Kingdom, she's worked with the Stealing Thunder Festival, Connection with Wonder, the Waterloo Festival, Elephant Tales, the Archive of Personal Stories, Miller's Way Project and many others. In Sweden, she's worked with *Sagobygden*/ Land of Legends, local schools and organisations.

She writes, gives talks and tells stories in English, Swedish, Norwegian and Spanish. When she isn't writing, performing or travelling, she can be found spending time with feline friends, working with the agency Love Cats (https://love-cats.uk/) in London.

For more information about her work see https://amhellbergmoberg.co.uk